MrPerfect.com

K.D Bloodworth

MrPerfect.com
K.D Bloodworth

Cover design by Classy Design

Edited by Big Bang Book Services

Thank you Kelley, Diane, Wendy, and my darling husband for all the encouragement and for believing in me. To my editor, Genevieve Scholl, who always forgives me for the many mistakes and encourages me. I'm a lucky woman.

Divorcing at fifty and starting over in Virginia is far from being the hardest challenge in Dawn's life. Overcoming the loneliness and feelings for her ex would prove even more difficult. One night, over too much wine, her friend Cindy fills out a profile for the online dating site, MrPerfect.com for her. It's not long until a virtual flirt turns into an every night cyber date with a handsome man in Montana.

Before the summer is over, Dawn finds herself hiking around the beautiful and wild front range of the Rockies, having a grand time and enjoying life again. Strange and weird things turn into terror forcing her to run for her life. Her only hope is to escape the madman and survive the wilderness. Lost and afraid, thirsty and hungry, she discovers her true courage and strength.

MrPerfect.com is a story of a woman's will to live and love again.

1

Montana

It was one crazy dream I was having. It was dark and I was cold, only it was late summer, so I shouldn't have been cold. My head was pounding like a world record hangover. I was way too old to be having a hangover like that. I didn't have that much to drink or maybe I did—I couldn't remember. My head really hurt, so I realized it wasn't really a dream. Crap. I moaned. That made me not want to open my eyes even more. As it turned out, I couldn't open them. It felt like someone had glued them shut. Reaching my hand up, I felt my eyes to make sure there was no glue and then tried again to pry them open. I finally got one eye open. The room wasn't so dark, now that I had bravely opened the other eye. I reached around the base of my neck to give myself some support and try to rise up. Where was I, anyway? I could make out some dusty furniture on the far wall, but not much else was visible. I was on a double size bed in the middle of what appeared to be a bedroom, and someone had spread an old quilt over the top of me.

I flipped the quilt over to the middle of the bed, swinging my feet over the edge and sitting up. The pounding in my head seemed to be fading. Maybe I was just asleep for too long. I knew that when I stayed in bed over eight hours my head and neck always seemed to hurt. Being fifty years old wasn't all fun and games.

As I placed my feet on the floor and dug my toes into the carpet, a flash of a memory came to me. I was having dinner. Dinner and wine. But I didn't remember finishing dinner or even going to bed. For that matter, I didn't remember the room at all. *Think, Dawn, think. What happened?*

I sat there for a good bit trying so hard to remember the night before, but my brain just would not focus. I tried to stand up, but I felt light headed and woozy; my stomach not liking the movement at all. Now I was feeling sick. There was a small trash can over by the dresser. I made a dash to the corner just in time as the leftover contents of my stomach left me. I was hanging onto the edge of the dresser and supporting myself with my right hand against the wall. Finally, after several more gut wrenching heaves, my stomach was empty. Now my head was pounding again. Feebly, I made it back over to the bed, carefully laying back down and pulling the quilt back over me. I felt warmer now. I felt myself falling into a peaceful sleep. I really should get up and figure out where I was or where Michael went off to.

That was his name! Michael! Michael, who? I was at his house. But when he gave me the tour of his home, I didn't remember this room. Crap, what was his last name? I needed to wake up. *Dawn, wake up. Wake up!* Sleep over takes me or I let myself drift away. This was all too confusing and I was so tired.

2

Montana

I opened my eyes again and the shades on the windows are now opened. I didn't even know people still put shades on their windows. The sun was shining into the room and I watched tiny particles of dust dancing in the light. I felt like I had been in bed for days. I was sweaty and in desperate need of a shower. Plus, I really needed to pee. Where was the bathroom? Looking around the room, I saw three doors. One needed to be a bathroom.

Throwing the quilt to the side, I noticed something different than the last time I had awoken. Or maybe it was a dream. I thought I remembered seeing a different quilt on the bed before. I was almost sure the quilt was green and brown, but this quilt was tan and brown with yellow. Did I dream of a different color?

As my feet hit the floor, a memory bounces back to me. I remembered getting sick. Yes, I was sick. I threw up in the trash can over in the corner by the dresser. Only now there was no trash can. Bathroom, I really needed a bathroom. The first door I opened was a closet. A closet with my clothes neatly hung on wooden hangers. My leather mules and my tennis shoes were on the floor sitting neatly side by side. Why didn't I remember putting my things in there? Whatever, I still needed a bathroom. I shut the closet door and walk over to another door.

I was happy to see a tiny half bath in what appeared to have once been another closet. After what seemed to be the longest relief ever in the history of women, I flushed the toilet and stepped over to the sink. I reached to turn on the water when I noticed my reflection in the small mirror.

Jesus! My hair! My hair had been cut! My hair was to my shoulders. It had taken me what seemed forever to grow my hair to that length so I could pull it up on top of my head. Now my highlighted hair was just long enough to cover my ears. Running my hands through what remained, I could feel the horrible chunks missing in the back. Fuck! Who did this to my head? Pulling the hair out from my skull on the sides with my fingers, I now could see what I would call a butcher's job on my hair. It would take forever for my slow growing hair to get over this crap. Who in the hell did this to me?

I pulled the door open with a vengeance, wanting to scream. Instead, I tear at the third door's doorknob. Grabbing the knob, I pulled with rage only to find the door was locked. I studied the brass plate around the doorknob, but there was no lock. I hadn't locked the door from the inside. Someone had locked me in the room. I began screaming and pounding on the door. "Hey! Let me out! Let me out!" No answer!

I stopped to listen to see if I could hear anyone. Nothing but silence. *Calm down, calm down. Catch your breath. You are not the kind of woman to panic. Breathe*, I kept telling myself, but the fear was grabbing at my throat. *Don't cry! No, don't cry. What good does crying do?* The words of my mom returned to me from so many years ago. The only thing crying did was make your eyes red and your nose run. I choked back the tears as I wiped my nose on my sleeve.

My sleeve! I swear I had on an elbow length shirt on the last time I looked. Or was it that dream again? I think I must be losing my mind.

There are two windows in the room. One on each side of the bed. Reaching the one on the left, I snapped the shade, making it fly up. It made several turns on the roller, making the pull handle flap against the glass. Jesus, there were bars on the window! I tried to open the single hung wooden framed window, but it wouldn't budge. Years of paint hold it shut. Then with a sinking feeling, I saw new nail heads on the window. The nail heads were flush with the window frame and sank into the side molding. Sticking my nose to the glass, I cupped my hands around my eyes to break the glare on the dirty glass. Trees surrounded the building. Tall Ponderosa Pines were my guess. I didn't know that much about western pines. The ground around the building and everything under the pines was bare of any grass. Lots of pine needles and sticks. I could make out large rocks under some of the pine needles. I saw no other signs of life, no birds, no animals and no walkways. I made my way over to the window on the right, flung the shade up, and found the same bars and nails. The view outside was the same. I was a prisoner? What kind of place was this? *Don't panic! Breathe.*

As calmly as I could, I walked over to the door and tried the handle again. To my surprise, it turned. I turned it slowly, trying not to make any noise. There was a slight click as the handle

11

released the bolt from the strike plate. I stopped and listened, holding my breath. Why was the door locked before and not now? Who unlocked it? Or maybe in my panic over my hair did I not turn the handle enough and the door was unlocked the whole time?

I slowly pulled the door open. I stood in the doorway, taking account of what lay before me. The walls of a large rectangle shaped room were logs. To the right, there was a small kitchen. Small but it seemed to be furnished with some dated but working appliances. There was even a toaster and microwave on the end counter. There was a large sink with a window above the back splash. The window was open, but there were bars on the outside of that window, too.

There was a small breakfast bar that separated the kitchen from a small wooden table with four chairs. There were two tall bar stools sitting at the bar. On the bar was a bowl of fruit. The fruit seemed to be fresh.

To the left of the doorway where I was still standing, was a stone fireplace with a large log hearth. In front of the fireplace was a large overstuffed leather sofa. On each side of the sofa, there were matching overstuffed leather chairs. Between the living room area and the dining table, on the wall directly in front of me, was a large wooden door. On each side of the door were more widows, again with bars on the outside.

I stepped out of the doorway, taking a step toward the door and realizing I was in my stocking feet. Damn it, my shoes were in the closet! Just as I started to turn to fetch my shoes, I heard someone stepping on what I thought sounded like a wooden platform, maybe a porch. I froze in my tracks as there was no place to run, no escape except for the door in front of me.

The door pushed open. Michael stood there holding an armful of logs cut in the right size for the fireplace. "Ah, you're awake." He smiled. Stepping inside, he shut the door behind him with his booted foot. He walked over to the left of the fireplace and placed the logs on top of another in a neatly stacked pile. Brushing his palms together, knocking the dirt and dust away, he turned toward me. "How long you been up? Are you hungry?"

"Where are we?" I managed to ask.

"Really? You don't remember the ride up here?" He flopped down in one of the leather chairs.

"Well, if I remembered I guess I wouldn't be asking, now would I?" My mind was racing, trying to remember anything.

"Jesus, I guess that wine and the couple of tokes on my pipe really did you in. I checked on you several times and decided to just let you sleep it off. Come sit down." He motioned toward the empty chair.

Walking over to the chair, I had the yearning to make a mad dash for the door. Instead, I eased my body into the leather, making no sudden moves for fear my head would start throbbing again.

"You want me to start a fire?" Michael was acting just like he had when I arrived at his house, one or two days ago. I had no idea how much time I had lost.

13

"A fire might be nice," I said as I drew my feet up on the edge of the chair, pulling my knees to my chest. "Just how long did I sleep? I really don't remember much of anything."

Michael started stacking the logs into the fireplace, not even looking my way. "You don't remember having dinner out on the patio? I thought for sure I made a meal worth remembering."

"I sort of remember you grilling steaks. Oh, and later we soaked in the hot tub."

"Yes, two really good rib eyes and a tossed salad. You made that while I grilled the steaks."

"But, what did we do after the hot tub? I just can't remember."

Michael had the fire roaring in no time. He settled back into his chair. "Well, we drank some more wine and we were talking about smoking pot. You said you hadn't smoked any pot since 1980 something. I offered you some and you said yes."

"I did?" I was having a very hard time believing that I would smoke pot, as I had sworn off the stuff years ago.

"You even said it had been so long since you had smoked any that it probably wouldn't even give you a buzz."

"I guess it did."

"And then some, I would say."

"Please fill me in."

Michael went into the kitchen, opened a bottle of white wine, and poured two glasses. He handed me one, took the other with him, and settled back into his chair. "Hair of the dog; drink up. Well, let's see. After we smoked the pipe up, we soaked for a bit more. You were laughing so hard I thought you might drown, so I talked you into getting out of the tub. Then you said you wanted to go for a ride. So I brought you up here to my cabin."

"Where are we?" I sipped my wine.

"My cabin is about twenty miles up in the mountains. Nice and quiet up here. I built it twenty years ago."

"Did I wake up once before today, or this afternoon, or whatever day it is?"

"You were pretty out of it by the time we got up here and it was dark. I put you to bed and decided to let you sleep it off."

"I think I remember waking up once, but I was sick. Did I throw up in a trash can?"

"Yes you did. When I checked on you again, you were passed out and in a cold sweat. So I changed you into some dry clothes and tucked you back under a clean quilt."

"Thanks. At least now I know that I didn't lose my mind. I thought I had dreamed all of that when I woke up a while ago. Why was the door locked? That really freaked me out."

"Oh, I'm so sorry. I had checked on you on my way out to cut some firewood. I was afraid you would leave if you woke up and I wasn't here."

"But then you unlocked it?"

"When I brought the first load of firewood in, I thought I heard you up so I unlocked the door. I went out to pick up the rest of the wood and found you standing in the doorway."

I took a sip of the wine and reached up to smooth my hair back. My hand hit the chopped up hair and I remembered. "MY HAIR! What the fuck happened to my hair?"

"Oh God, you really don't remember anything. You did that. Not me!"

"What? You are trying to tell me I chopped my own hair up like this?"

"Yes. Before we left the house, you decided you wanted your hair short again. You found a pair of scissors in my desk and started cutting. You were laughing. I swear it wasn't me."

"Jesus, what kind of pot did you give me? This is fucking crazy."

"It's okay. When we go back down to town, you can get it trimmed up."

"I could really use a shower."

"Door to the right. There are towels and the things you brought with you on the shelf. Take your time; I'm going to fix something to eat."

I walked into the bathroom and shut the door behind me, noticing there was no lock. There was an old claw foot tub with an overhead shower. There was a shelf with soaps, bubble bath, and special scented oils. The shelves on the side of the pedestal sink were full of big fluffy towels. My things had been placed very neatly on the shelf right above the sink.

Looking in the mirror at my chopped up hair, I was thinking that none of this was making any sense at all. Really, I would never cut my own hair. I might trim my bangs once in a great while, but this was ridiculous. I was not sure that I would ever smoke pot again. How did I get into this, anyway? What was I thinking?

3

Virginia

"I don't know, Cindy; I'm happy just the way things are. I don't want to go on one of those dating sites. You know what kind weirdoes are on there?"

"Gee, thanks, you know that's how Ted and I met?" Cindy laughed.

"You're one of the lucky ones!" I turned back to my computer.

I had known Cindy for almost two years. She was one of the first people I had made friends with when I came to Richmond to work. I had been on vacation visiting family in the Richmond area when I noticed an ad in the Richmond Times for an auditor. The same work I was doing in Alabama, only the Richmond job paid twice as much. Deciding that it couldn't hurt, I filled out the application and attached my updated resume. I smiled as I hit the send button. Who knows, something may happen before I had to catch the plane back to Birmingham. I was in a dead end at the job I was holding in Alabama.

There was another reason I hated the thought of going back to Birmingham. The ex-husband was still there and I had the unfortunate timing of running into him several times a week. After the divorce, I had moved to Birmingham to get away from him and his new girlfriend. However, the new girlfriend lived in Birmingham and not that far from my workplace.

No matter what I did, the memories were always there. John was my second husband. Vietnam had put a sudden stop to my first marriage. I found myself a widow at the young age of twenty four. That had broken my heart to the point I gave up on finding love. It was after all the early Seventies and I was having too much fun. I preferred footloose and fancy free and I intended to keep it that way. Back then there were no computers, no dating sites, just the old fashion way of meeting people, at bars, through friends, or believe it or not, at the grocery store. My girlfriends and I were having lots of fun meeting men, dancing the nights away and occasionally waking up with a handsome stranger.

We were all from the same area, growing up around Ann Arbor and meeting each other working at the bank. There were three of us; Joan, Patty and yours truly. We worked in the downtown branch of Bank of Michigan. Working Monday through Friday, we partied hard back in those days. Employers were not giving drug tests back then, so we indulged more than we should have— too much beer, too much wine, and some good home grown pot. There was no shortage of pot in Ann Arbor in those days.

Saturdays we had a standing date for brunch down at the local Big Boy to nurse our hangovers, compare notes from Friday night, and maybe discuss a date we had made for Saturday night. One of those Saturday morning brunches had always stuck in my mind.

We were sitting in our favorite booth, sipping coffee and enjoying our first smoke of the day.

"Geese, I think I smoked enough last night for all three of us," I said as I blew smoke rings up toward the ceiling.

"I know what you mean. Why do I smoke so much if I'm drinking?" Patty laughed as she lit another cigarette. Patty smoked more than any of us. She was the oldest by several years. She had also been single the longest of the group.

Joan, on the other hand, was a bit older than me but younger than Patty, divorced longer than I had been widowed, but divorced a shorter time than Patty. We teased her about being in the middle of everything. She only smoked after noon and when she was out drinking. But on Saturdays, she would break down and smoke before noon.

Patty took a long drag from her cigarette and blew out, "Did you all see that guy I was dancing with last night?"

We did but neither one of us could remember for sure what he looked like.

"He looked like John Norman Collins!"

"No way!" Joan reached for one of my cigarettes.

Ann Arbor had not been long over the killings of co-eds that John Norman Collins had committed. Just the mentioning of his name still made most girls in the area shiver with fear.

"He did. It freaked me out. I was coming back from the bathroom and he approached me, asking if I wanted to go someplace else. He was sort of grabby out on the dance floor, but I thought he was just a little drunk. I told him I was waiting for my date."

"Jesus, Patty, why didn't you say something?" I had goose bumps even though I knew Collins was in jail.

"When I said I was waiting for my date, he disappeared." Patty poured us all some more coffee.

"You know, there could be more guys like him out there, Collins that is," Joan whispered. "Maybe we should be more careful."

"Crap, he disappeared; maybe he kidnapped another girl!" I was freaking myself out.

"He wasn't a killer or kidnapper. I don't think, anyway." Patty started to laugh and for some crazy reason, Joan and I did, too. We never did start being more careful. Now I'm wondering if that conversation had come back to haunt me.

4

Montana

Enough of that kind of thinking. I grabbed some bubble bath, poured too much into the tub, turned on the water full blast, and watched as a mountain of fluffy bubbles reached for the ceiling. I shed my clothes and slipped into the hot water. Taking a big breath, I slid under the water, staying there with my eyes shut until I had to come up for air.

Wiping the bubbles from my face and eyes, I reached forward to turn off the water. "Shit! You scared the crap out of me!" I screeched. Michael was standing with his head poked in the bathroom.

"Sorry, sorry! I just wanted to know if you wanted rice with our pork chops."

"Rice is fine. Whatever you want to fix." I was completely covered with bubbles, feeling as if I was dressed and no need to cover myself. Michael turned and closed the door behind him.

Creepy; this was getting creepy. Or maybe I was just creeping myself out. If he was going to do anything creepy or offensive to me, he had plenty of time. I need to get a grip.

I was done soaking and most of the bubbles were gone when a call from the kitchen got my attention. "Ten minutes until dinner!"

"Okay!" I shouted back. I pulled the plug from the drain, turned the water on, flipping the lever to allow the shower to run. The water was cold at first. Then the hot water kicked in, my goose bumps disappeared, and I rinsed the remaining bubbles away. I wrapped my head and body in towels from the shelf, picked up my dirty clothes, and tiptoed to the bedroom where I had been sleeping.

I grabbed some clean underwear, a sweatshirt, and some blue jeans. I ran my fingers through my towel dried hair, trying to fluff what was left of it, which didn't feel like much. Then I opened the door to the wonderful smell of dinner being served at the kitchen bar.

"Wow that smells wonderful." I pulled a stool out and sat down. Before me were pork chops, rice, green beans, apple sauce, white wine, and some kind of hot rolls. I eyeballed the glass of wine, wondering if I should drink any more.

"Nothing fancy. Hope it tastes as good as it smells." Michael was smiling as he picked up his glass of wine and held it as if to make a toast. "To a great week."

I clicked my glass to his and then took a tiny sip. *Yum, Riesling, my favorite.* "Let's eat."

I found myself enjoying the dinner and the small talk. The Riesling was probably too good, as I had started on my third glass when Michael stood up. "You should go enjoy the fire while I clean up the kitchen."

"Oh, I can help; after all, you did all the cooking." As I stood up, I felt light headed. Oh no, too much wine again. "Wow, I think I drank a little too much wine. Maybe I will go sit down."

"No worries. It will only take me a couple of minutes to clean this up. I clean while I cook."

I took a seat on the sofa, tucked my legs up under me, and leaned my upper body on the overstuffed end. I laid my head in the crook of my arm, enjoying the warm glow from the fire. My face was feeling warm and flushed. My eyes were heavy. I was trying very hard to be a polite guest, but I couldn't keep my eyes open. I didn't even remember actually falling asleep.

When opening my eyes to a bright sunny bedroom, I did remember being carried into the bedroom and someone laying me on the bed. I was pretty sure it was Michael, but I couldn't swear to that fact. It must have been him. I was in his cabin, after all.

Gee, Dawn, you really can't hold your wine anymore, I was thinking to myself. I peeled the quilt off of me, swung my feet out of the bed and onto the floor. Well, at least I still had on the same pair of jeans and shirt. No one changed my clothes for me this time. The shades on the windows were up and I could see it was a beautiful sunny day outside. I walked quietly over to the door, almost afraid to try the handle, but it pulled open freely.

"There you are. I thought you were going to sleep all day." Michael was sitting in one of the chairs reading a newspaper. "Not much but gloom and doom in the paper. It is several days old. You want to read it?"

"No thanks, but I could use some coffee." I walked over to the front door, opening the heavy wood door. A fresh mountain breeze gently blew

24

through the screen door. "Boy that smells good." I turned around to Michael holding a cup of coffee toward me. I took it greedily, taking a big drink.

I walked over and took a seat on the stool where I had sat the night before. "I guess I really crashed and burned last night. I guess the fire made me sleepy."

"You were out of it by the time I finished the dishes. I put you to bed later." Michael poured himself a cup of coffee and sat down beside me. "You want to go for a hike today?"

"That sounds great. Let me put some shoes on first." I finished my coffee and ran to the bathroom. I was washing my face when I noticed what appeared to be a bruise on my neck. I stretched over the sink, closer to the mirror to get a better look. I couldn't tell if it was a bruise or a tiny hickey. I couldn't think of how I could have gotten either. I finished my business in the bathroom, put some shoes and socks on, and grabbed a jacket from the closet.

"Ready?" Michael stood at the front door dressed for a hike in the woods. As he slipped a lightweight flannel shirt over his T-shirt, I noticed he had a handgun stuffed in the back of his waistband. He picked up a backpack and slung it over one shoulder.

"Ready. Oh, do we have some water to take with us?"

"Sure do." He handed me a fanny pack that had two little water bottles attached to the sides. I slipped it around my waist. "Let's go."

Stepping out on the front porch, I was amazed at the view that greeted me. We were surrounded by huge Ponderosa Pines, but there was what I would consider a rather small front yard covered with a bit of green grass. Then I noticed there was no driveway leading up to the cabin. There were several paths leading in different directions away from the cabin. They all looked to be well traveled, one no more than the other. To the right of the porch was a small structure, more like a lean-to that held several cords of cut wood.

There was a path straight ahead of us, leading off into the woods. I could see that it curved to the right about ten yards into the trees. There were two more paths off to the left. I couldn't see too far down either one of them. One thing I did notice was that not one of the paths showed a parking area with a vehicle in sight.

"Where's the car?" I couldn't help but wonder.

"Oh, it's down the path a bit. We can't drive up here. I still need to cut a driveway from the end of the road. I can drive in from the back side, but it's an extra twenty miles from the house in town." Michael was walking ahead of me, heading to the path straight ahead of us. For some reason, I just assumed that was where the car would be, so I didn't ask which path led to the car.

"Wow, when you said you had a cabin in the mountains, I didn't think it would be this remote. How far are we from town?"

"Which town?"

"Great Falls, where I flew into." I was trying to remember if he had told me how far it was in one of our conversations, but there was no memory there.

"About sixty five miles from there, but only about twenty miles from Augusta, as a crow flies." He smiled, turned, and started into the woods.

I followed, thinking I should be enjoying the beautiful mountain scenery, but my mind kept recalling how we had hooked up.

5

Virginia

One afternoon Cindy stopped by my desk. "It's fifteen minutes until go home time. It's Friday! Let's go have a drink after work. Ted had to go up to D.C. today and he won't be back until really late. Girls night out!"

"I don't know, I should really......"

"Yes you should really get out! I promise I will not let us get into any trouble." She smiled, winked, and turned toward her desk.

"What the hell? I'll go."

"About time." Cindy laughed.

Thirty minutes later, we were down in what was known as the bottoms of Richmond, having a glass of wine. The place was packed with all the young professionals that worked in and around the city. I had been out with Cindy several times before so this was nothing new. We would chat for a while, order something to eat, and then she would go home to Ted and I would go home to a good book and some more wine.

We had decided on pizza. After we had our share, Cindy asked for a box to take the leftovers to Ted for a midnight snack. "Hey, Ted won't be home probably until after midnight. Why don't you come over? We can crawl into another bottle of wine. You can spend the night, so I don't have to worry about you driving home."

"Oh, I should probably get home."

"Why?"

She was right. There was nothing and no one there.

"You can jump into some of my sweats and a T shirt. I even have some new guest's toothbrushes you can use. No excuses."

I finally gave in, "Okay."

Cindy lived in an upscale neighborhood of Richmond, just across what was known as the Nickel Bridge that cost twenty five cents to cross. No one remembered when the fare went up from a nickel so the name stuck.

Like most homes in Richmond, Cindy lived in a remodeled Colonial. Once a two story box with wood siding, it was now a two story brick with added wings to each side of the original box. The driveway leading to the unattached carriage house was cobblestone and just like the many alleys in the city there was green moss growing between most of the old stones. Her yard was landscaped old Richmond style with lots of Azaleas, Magnolias, and other colorful blooming plants. There was a cobblestone walkway leading up to the back door, which opened to a mudroom.

The mudroom led to a huge kitchen, designed to look old but was very much equipped with up to the date, modern stainless steel appliances, cherry cupboards, and dark granite. There was under the cupboard lighting that had been left on, making the room glow.

In the middle of the room was an island with a small sink on one end, a wine cabinet in the middle, and seating on the other end that was designed as an eating bar. I set my purse on the island and pulled a cherry wood stool out from the bar. Cindy reached into the wine cabinet and pulled out a bottle of Riesling. Under one of the cabinets hung a collection of different shaped wine glasses. I grabbed two while Cindy opened the bottle.

She poured two glasses, almost full, and slid one in front of me. "You are spending the night. Drink up."

I laughed, holding my glass up for a toast "To good friends."

"To good friends," she repeated and we both took a long drink and laughed some more.

We sat and chatted about work and things she wanted to finish with the house next summer. All was depending on Ted's job. He wanted to find something where he didn't have to travel to Washington so often, but the pay was great. He had this job when they met four years ago.

Cindy and Ted both had been married before. Ted's first wife had died. He had no children. Cindy, like me had been in a bad marriage for ten years and finally divorced the creep, as she always referred to him. Cindy didn't have any children either. Cindy and Ted were both into their forties and were pretty sure they didn't want any children. They were happy the way things were.

Half way through the second bottle of wine, with our hair down, shoes off, and blouses pulled out of our skirts, Cindy pulled out her laptop. "I think we should go on-line and build you a profile on Mr. Perfect."

"What the hell is Mr. Perfect?" I laughed. "No such thing!"

"Ted would disagree with you." Cindy took another drink of wine and tapped away on the computer.

"Is that the website that you and Ted met on? What did he look under, Ms. Perfect?"

"Look at me, of course he did!" Cindy was laughing so hard she could hardly type.

"Well, you have a point there. You are pretty awesome."

"Here we go. Sign up for an account. Let's build your profile just for kicks and giggles and see what happens. You don't have to answer anyone if you don't want to."

I had just enough wine in me to say, "Oh hell, why not?"

Cindy started typing:

User ID: Delta Dawn

"Wasn't that your old CB name when you were driving truck?"

"Yes"

"Password?"

"How about DD50?" I could remember that—Delta Dawn and my age.

"I'll add that photo you showed me the other day. The one taken at your place, where you are wearing that pretty blue blouse and you're holding a glass of wine."

"Okay, that's a pretty good photo, I guess."

I stood there while Cindy filled out the questionnaire. She knew a lot about me since we chatted every day at work over lunch.

"Let's see if I got this all right. Interests, I listed, hiking, shooting, hunting, fishing, and riding my Harley or any outdoor activity. Want to add anything?"

"Nope, I think that just about sums me up."

Cindy hit the accept button and I watched as my personal information went into cyberspace. Was there really a Mr. Perfect out there for me? I doubted it, but Cindy was sure there was.

"I need to eat something. I have had way too much wine. You hungry?"

I finished the last drop of wine in my glass. "Not really, but I probably should eat something, too."

Cindy pulled some cheese from the double door refrigerator and some crackers from one of the pantries. She poured us some more wine. We sat there nibbling at the cheese and crackers and drinking more wine when her laptop chimed. "Well, well, what do we have here?" Cindy pulled the laptop over, sitting it between us. "Hey, you have a hit!"

"Really?" I couldn't believe it.

"Check this out. He looks like Grizzly Adams!"

There before me was a profile of a man probably in his late fifties with a photo of himself standing in front of some trees. "He does look like Grizzly Adams, but not as handsome."

Cindy tapped away on the computer. "He's from Georgia. Ooh, a Southern Grizzly Adams."

"There are no Grizzlies in Georgia."

"Never mind," Cindy announced. "He's married and looking for someone to join him and his wife."

"See, I told you; creeps! Can you undo my profile?" I poured more wine.

"Oh, don't give up so easy. You have to kiss a lot of frogs before you find your prince." She tapped some more keys.

"More like my Princes always turn out to be scum bags."

"Ah, here's another profile."

I was standing behind Cindy, looking over her shoulder. "He looks too young. He must be sixteen! I don't want jail bait!"

"Profile says he's twenty five. That might be fun to play with!"

"I don't think so."

I was just about to sit back down when another hit on my profile came into view. The photo came into focus and I just stood there, unable to comment. Looking back at us from the laptop was a green eyed man, dressed in what I would consider bird hunting attire, brown pants and brown hunting jacket. In front of him sat a black Labrador retriever. The man was holding an over and under shotgun. There was something lying on the ground in front of the Lab, but the photo was cut off. "Read the profile!"

Cindy started reading aloud, "Fifty-four years old, six foot four. Divorced, grown children, one granddaughter. Lives in Montana. He's a gunsmith. Likes shooting, hunting, hiking, fishing, camping, and most anything outdoors. He loves his wilderness cabin. His name is Michael Conrad."

"Gee, he's handsome. But Montana? That's across the country."

"So what? Will it hurt to ping him back? It's not like he's going to show up on your doorstep." Without another word, Cindy pinged his profile back. "Maybe he will answer you."

Just as I was about to answer her, the backdoor opened. We both jumped and started laughing. Ted walked into the kitchen shaking his head. "What are you two up to?"

"I got Dawn on Mr. Perfect and we thought you were her new contact showing up. Not really, he's in Montana."

Ted set his briefcase down, hugged and kissed Cindy, and gave me a friendly hug. "How much wine have you two had?"

"Oh, probably too much. Maybe you should put us to bed," Cindy giggled.

The computer pinged again. It was Montana. We all read the text. "Delta Dawn, you have time to chat?"

"Answer him!" Cindy giggled.

"I don't know what to say. I'm ready for bed." I really was ready for bed with too much wine under my belt.

"Just say you were about to get off the computer for the night. Maybe you can chat tomorrow night."

I took over the keyboard and typed just that. Within a couple of seconds, the reply came. "How about eight tomorrow night, your time?"

Laughing, I typed back, "Sure, I'll look for you, good night." I shut the computer before he could reply. "I really need to go to bed."

The three of us made it upstairs, Cindy handing me a T-shirt and a pair of sweat pants. She pointed me toward the guest bedroom.

"Good night; see ya in the morning," I offered as I closed the door. I changed clothes and fell into bed. Cindy was right; I had too much wine. I left one foot on the floor to keep the room from spinning. I knew I was going to have a terrible headache in the morning.

***

I was right; my aching head woke me up before the sunlight coming into the bedroom window did. I rolled over onto my back, thinking my head was going to bust open. I had always thought nothing was as bad as a wine hangover, but now I was sure. Yikes my head was pounding with every heartbeat. I gently got out of bed and headed to the hallway bathroom. I passed a mirror above the sink on the way to the toilet. "Holy crap," I murmured as I glanced at myself. "Death warmed over."

After I relieved myself, I washed my face with some cool water. I needed some coffee, but I dreaded the trip down the stairs. I was sure each step was going to be painful. I took my time making it to the bottom landing. Each step felt like someone was hitting me with a sledge hammer in the temple. I rounded the corner from the hallway to the kitchen to find Cindy sitting at the bar, holding her head with both hands. Ted was whistling as he stood at the range frying bacon.

"Stop that damn whistling," Cindy moaned.

I started to laugh, but that only caused more pain in my head. I had tried to open my eyes fully, only to find that let in too much light. "I agree; stop!"

Ted poured both of us large mugs of coffee. The hot liquid helped get rid of my furry mouth.

"You girls look like you had a large time last night. You were pretty funny when I got home." He pointed to the three empty wine bottles. "Oh, that laptop has been chirping all morning."

"What time is it?!" I looked at my watch, but it was blurry.

"Almost noon." Ted was just too cheery.

Cindy pushed the laptop over to me, flipping it open. The Mr. Perfect site was still up on the screen. I decided to send Montana a question. I started typing. "What kind of dinner was lying on the ground in front of you and the dog? The over and under is a twelve gauge Browning?"

All of a sudden I got a ping and an answer. "Of all the questions I have been asked on this web site, I have never been asked that one. Dinner was pheasant and the shotgun was indeed a Browning."

I took a long drink of my coffee and answered, "I grew up hunting small game, so I figured it was pheasant or duck. Nice looking hunting dog, too."

We chatted back and forth on-line for almost twenty minutes. Ted was serving breakfast when I excused myself from Montana. "I need to get off of here; breakfast is being served. It was nice chatting with you."

"My pleasure. Will you meet me back on-line later? Say about eight, your time?"

"That would be fun; I will chat with you later." I closed the application and shut the lid to the laptop. Ted set a plate full of eggs, biscuits, bacon, and grits in front of me. I looked up and both he and Cindy were smiling at me. "What?" I smiled back.

6

Montana

We walked along the mountain path which snaked its way laterally along the top of a ridge. I stayed a good ten feet behind Michael so that I didn't get smacked in the face with any branches he might have pushed aside. Every now and then he would stop and ask me if I was doing okay, then we would continue down the path. I thought we were heading north, but in the tall trees I wasn't so sure. I was thinking we must have hiked over a mile when Michael stopped. I caught up with him to see an opening in the trees. Before us lay a high mountain meadow, surrounded by tall pines and huge granite looking boulders. The meadow was full of tall green grass and some kind of tiny yellow flowers. The sky was a brilliant blue. The sun was slightly to my back and left. I had been right; we were walking north.

"This is one of my favorite places in the whole world." Michael smiled and took my hand, leading me out into the meadow.

"This is beautiful. Makes ya feel like we are the only people that have ever seen this."

"I would venture to say not many others know of this place. As many times as I have been up here, I have never run into anyone." He stopped, let go of my hand, and set his backpack on the ground. He opened the pack, pulled a lightweight blanket out and spread it on the ground. He pulled several containers from the pack. "Lunch is served."

I sat down on the blanket and took a long drink from one of the water bottles. There was cheese, grapes, crackers, and some kind of cookies in the containers.

"You see many bears around here?"

"Yes, a few, depending on the time of the year."

"So the pistol, is it big enough for a bear? Just in case?"

"I have never had a problem with the bears. Mostly they see me and take off in the other direction. I carry the pistol for people and bear spray for the bears."

"People?" I wasn't sure if I felt safe or scared.

"Don't worry; just a precaution in case we should run up on a stupid poacher. They get stupid if they get caught."

I laid back and let the sun warm my body. This place was as beautiful as Michael had said in our four months of texting, emailing, and phone conversations. Why anyone would want to live any place else was a mystery to me. From the minute I stepped out of the terminal in Great Falls, I was in love with Montana. Now, lying in the meadow, the sun warming me down to my bones, the air sweet, fresh and the sound of mountain birds in the distance, I understood why people did whatever they could to live here.

I felt Michael reclining beside me. I opened my eyes to see him close, lying on his side, his head propped up on one hand and smiling. "Can I kiss you?"

"Well, are you a mind reader, too? I was hoping...." But before I could finish, he leaned over and gently kissed me. A soft, tender kiss. The kind of kiss that made a woman want more. I kissed back. It had been a very long time since I had been kissed. I reached up and ran my fingers through his sun kissed brown hair. Michael wore his hair cut fairly short, but still enough to run my fingers through. He was slightly grey on the temples. Just enough to make him have that distinguished look about him. As I ran my fingers through his hair, he kissed me a tiny bit harder, this time allowing his tongue to slip over my bottom lip. I felt a warm rush run up through the middle of my body, almost taking my breath away. My first thought was how silly this was. After all, we were both over fifty. But that thought vanished as fast as it appeared.

I got brave enough to allow my tongue to find his in response. I think this took him by surprise just a bit as I felt him take in a little extra air. My next thought was that maybe this ole gal still had it after all, but I wasn't sure if I was ready to give myself completely.

I pulled my hands from his hair, placing one on each shoulder then pushed gently. There was no resistance. Michael broke the kiss. "Enough?" He was smiling at me.

"I don't know if I'm ready yet." I laughed. "Okay, physically I'm ready, but I don't know if I'm mentally ready."

"No worries, we're not going anywhere for another week. I can wait until you are ready, as long as you still don't think I'm an axe murderer. I've been waiting since you agreed to visit me." Michael stood, smiled, and took a drink of water. I was well aware of his excitement as I scanned his tall frame in the sunlight.

He handed me the water bottle. "Come on; there's something I want to show you. It's a bit of a hike, but it's worth the trip."

We gathered up the scattered remains of the lunch and packed up the blanket. Michael put the backpack on and I clipped the fanny pack back on my waist. He took my hand and guided me toward the far right corner of the meadow.

"Not long ago, I was up here walking and spotted a grizzly standing at the edge of the meadow, sniffing the air and watching me. I started singing and it took off into the woods. Keep an eye out and talk at full volume. We don't want to surprise any residents."

My only knowledge of bear country was from reading and the Discovery Channel. Since Michael had lived here for almost thirty years, I was putting my trust in him.

7

Virginia

Just before eight that evening after an afternoon of nursing my wine head back to health, I sat down on the sofa in my tiny studio apartment in Richmond. I considered it tiny as the whole apartment would fit in my living room in the house that John and I had once shared. The first floor apartment in a four unit building housed a galley kitchen, a great room of sorts that could hold a love seat, one small chair and a two person dinette set. The bedroom held a double sized bed and one dresser, leaving only enough room to squeeze between the bed and wall enabling me to change the bedding. The tiny bathroom held the toilet, a pedestal sink, and a thirty-six inch square shower. There were two closets in the place, which was a huge plus. The best thing was it had off street parking, which was a big deal in Richmond. It was also within walking distance to anything my heart desired on my off time.

Eight o'clock came and I opened up my page on Mr. Perfect. I checked, but there were no notices popping up on my computer. Just about the time I was closing the lid on the laptop, thinking what a silly fool I had been, my laptop pinged. My heart sort of jumped into my throat. Mr. Perfect conversation screen popped up.

"Hey, Delta Dawn, are you there?" I watched the words appear on my screen.

"Yes. I was about to sign out."

"I was outside with Jake and he decided to hunt down a grouse. You have time to chat?"

"Yes. Is Jake is the black Lab in your photo?"

"Yes; he's my pal and the best dog I have ever had."

The conversation started there and before I knew it, it was eleven. Not once had I yawned, which surprised me because I was usually in bed by ten. We touched on just about everything, including our failed marriages.

Michael was born and raised in Tennessee and had been a county Deputy up near Chattanooga for almost ten years. His wife decided she liked his partner better and they divorced when his daughter was eight. Not wanting to spend so much time away from his daughter, he went to gunsmith school and started his own business. He said that life got so dangerous around Chattanooga that he decided to move to Montana where there was less crime. His daughter had moved with him and graduated from high school, then moved back to Tennessee. He had been single all those years and wanted to stay that way.

I filled him in on my bad marriage to John, also a cop. How John's job had become more important than anything else in his life. How we lived like roommates instead of husband and wife. Then he had the affair with a co-worker while I was in Richmond. We divorced shortly after that. There wasn't much else to explain.

"So, do you like living in Richmond?"

"That's a good question. I like it better than Alabama or I wouldn't have moved here."

"Well, I suppose that makes a good bit of sense."

"I bet you are laughing. I have enjoyed this evening, but I need to get off this thing. I need to get up fairly early and get things ready for work on Monday."

"Okay, I will give you a ping tomorrow about the same time if that's alright with you?"

"Sure. Will hook up tomorrow. Have a good night."

"Goodnight." The conversation popup screen disappeared. I signed out of MrPerfect.com.

I stepped out onto the front stoop of the apartment building and lit a cigarette. I had quit smoking years ago, but picked them back up during the divorce. I only smoked once in a while and this seemed to be like a good time. Lighting the cigarette, I took a deep drag and let the smoke escape. I still felt guilty that I had started the old nasty habit again. Maybe it was just nerves or having a conversation with a man over two thousand miles away. I supposed that was safe enough, but who was I kidding? I knew nothing about this man. He could have been an axe murderer for all I knew.

I finished my cigarette, crushed the butt, picked up the remains of the filter, and let myself back into the apartment. Tossing the butt into the garbage, I noticed my cell phone flashing. I had a message. I looked at the phone to see a missed call from Cindy. Thinking I should call her back, I decided to wait until tomorrow. I headed to bed.

Sleep eluded me as my thoughts were of a man I didn't really know. Just words on a popup screen on my computer. I felt silly. I wasn't a teenager or even a young woman and yet, for the first time in a very long time, I was feeling attractive. The last time I looked at the alarm clock it was reading almost three.

***

My eyes popped open before seven. Crap, I was too old to be running on four hours of sleep. I tried to fall back asleep, but finally gave up just before eight. I got up and put a pot of coffee on to brew. Just as I poured a mug full, my cell phone rang. I knew it would be Cindy before I looked at the screen.

"Morning Cindy," I answered.

"Ah, good, you are up! Tell me, tell me!"

"Tell you what?" I laughed.

"Come one; he texted you, no?" Cindy sounded more excited than I did.

"Yes." I was going to make her drag information out of me for just a bit.

"Well? Geez, Dawn, give me some details!"

Over two cups of coffee and one cigarette, I gave her the details of the texting conversation from the night before. As I was telling her, I remembered a few things that he said that didn't make much sense now. A comment about a cabin up in the mountains he had built for exciting adventures. He must have been talking about hunting or hiking.

"Are you going to contact him again?" There was hope in Cindy's question.

"He said he would contact me again tonight about eight. We'll see."

"Well, this is a good start. Sort of like Ted and I started. Look what a jewel Ted turned out to be. Speaking of which, he just got up, so I need to go make us some breakfast. Want to join us?"

"No thanks; I need to get the laundry done, things ready for the work week. After all I have an on-line date tonight." We both laughed.

***

Again just before eight, I was on my sofa with my laptop, on-line and waiting for a ping from Mr. Perfect. To my surprise, I had two flirts waiting on me when I opened my profile. I quickly read each message. One was from a local Virginia man. His profile said he was sixty three, single, and looking for a long term relationship. The second flirt was from a younger man by the looks of his photo. He lived and worked in the D.C. area. I disregarded both just as I got a ping from Michael. I felt a smile come to my face.

"Hey Michael," I typed before he had a chance to respond. "How was your day?"

"Hey. It was okay. I had taken an old friend of mine up to the cabin to spend the day but things didn't work out like I had planned. I ended up spending most of the day up there alone after I got the mess cleaned up. How was your day?"

At the time I didn't think much of his remark about the old friend and the mess. I was too new at this to ask questions that needed to be asked. Instead, I told him about my rather boring day of house work, laundry, and a short bike ride around the city before noon. Businesses opened up around noon and traffic became a problem. I really needed some excitement in my mind-numbing existence.

We ended up texting until almost midnight. I was having fun at this new game. A safe game in my mind because what could happen with me in Virginia and him in Montana?

"Michael, it's almost midnight and I need to get up early in the morning for work. I really need to sign off."

"I didn't realize it was that late. I will let you go. I'll talk to you tomorrow. Good night."

"Good Night."

***

Five thirty came much too soon, but I did make it to work in time with time allowing me to chat with Cindy over a cup of coffee before we fired up the computers. When she walked into the lunch room, she smiled. "Wow, did you sleep at all last night or were you on the computer with Montana all night?"

Dee, one of the other women in the office was pouring herself a cup of coffee turned to me. "Who is Montana?"

"Dawn's new love interest," Cindy blurted out.

"Not a love interest; just a guy I meant on-line. No big deal." I looked at my watch and was happy to see it was eight and time to get to our desks. I didn't have to explain anything. I turned and walked out of the break room, leaving Cindy and Dee wondering.

8

Montana

We walked beside each other until we got to the edge of the meadow. I looked back over my shoulder and realized we had been walking up hill on a slight grade. Right at the edge of the meadow I noticed a patch of ground about six feet long and three feet wide that appeared freshly dug up. No grass, no rocks, just brown dirt. I thought that seemed out of place. As we left the tall grass, the ground became covered with pine needles and small mountain underbrush. There were also large boulders of Rocky Mountain granite making what was left of the trail zig zag. The trees loomed over us, blocking out most of the sun. Every so often a shaft of sunlight broke through the treetops, lighting the forest.

"This is so beautiful." I stopped to take a photo with my phone. I reached into the fanny pack, but my phone was not there. "Crap, where's my phone?"

"Ah, no signal up here. I took it out before we left the cabin. No sense in packing things we don't need."

"Oh," I tried to remember when he had an opportunity to handle the fanny pack. "I was going to take a picture."

"You'll have another opportunity for photos. Come on." Michael smiled, turned, and started walking.

We walked for almost an hour, through thick underbrush, tall trees, a few open places and a couple trickles of mountain water making its way down hill. We had turned so many times; I had no sense of direction, again trusting my guide.

Michael stopped periodically, allowing me to catch up with him. I could hear the rumble of water, loud and close. I was watching where I was stepping since the ground was covered with rocks and moss, making the going slippery. When I stopped beside of him, I looked up to see a thirty foot waterfall, dropping into a creek just below our feet. The sun was shining on the waterfall, causing the mist to look like diamonds falling from the sky. I stepped to the right just a bit and the sunlight hitting the mist displayed a tiny rainbow.

I turned around to see Michael sitting on a large log. He was grinning at me.

"What?" I asked.

"Oh, I was just enjoying you appreciating the falls. Pretty nice, huh?"

"It's just beautiful. You were right; well worth the hike." I sat down beside him on the log, took the water bottle from the fanny pack, and we shared a drink.

"It's getting late; we should start back."

I put the water bottle away and started to stand. Michael held his hand out to help me up; when I reached full height, he pulled me close to him and kissed me. The first time he kissed me I had thought the reason for my hot rush response was that I hadn't been kissed in so very long. This time I realized it just wasn't that, but it was the fact this man really knew how to kiss and then some. I found myself on my tiptoes, kissing him back. He pulled me closer. I could feel the heat between us. I didn't want to stop, but I broke the kiss.

"You have the nicest mouth, soft and kissable lips," he whispered. "Lips that should be kissed often."

I cocked my head upward. "Thank you." I kissed him quickly. "You said we needed to head back to the cabin."

I turned to head back the way we came, but Michael whistled at me. "This way."

We walked along the creek for what seemed like a couple of miles; then we turned right and started up a long hill. There was no path that I could make out. Michael walked ahead of me with confidence, not needing a trail. I could tell the sun was setting from the pink glow of light coming through the massive pines.

"Michael, I need to take a breather. Do you mind?" I had stopped and got one of the water bottles from the pack.

"Of course not, but we can't stop for too long. It gets dark quickly up here. There are things out here in the night that we don't want to deal with."

"Is that why there are bars on the cabin windows?" I had wanted to ask him that before, but I didn't seem to be able to find the right time. At dinner the night before would have been awkward. "Pass the pork chops, please. Oh and by the way, why do you have bars on the windows?" That just didn't seem like good timing.

"Yes, that and cabins have been broken into up here. Mostly kids from the city out screwing around."

That didn't answer my question about what the things were. I was about to ask him to elaborate on what he meant about things in the night, but he grabbed my hand and coached me onward.

I had no idea where we were, what direction we were walking, or if we were even close to the cabin. It was now getting dusk and with the tall pines all around us it seemed even darker. I heard a coyote off in the distance, but I couldn't tell from what direction. I was on the verge of getting freaked out when we broke into a clearing. There just a few yards ahead of us was the cabin. I felt relief run through my body.

"I'm going to start the generator. You want to take a shower before dinner?" He stepped under a little lean-to behind the cabin and started the generator. Several lights inside the cabin came on, making the place look more inviting.

"That would be nice, but I can help with dinner and shower later." I stepped up on the front porch when a feeling of desolation ran up my back. I turned to see the very last glimmers of daylight disappear, leaving the area totally dark.

Michael stepped up on the porch behind me. "Something wrong?"

"No, just listening to the dead silence. Seems odd after leaving Richmond where there is never much quiet."

"It's even more quiet here than in Augusta, if ya can believe that." Michael headed for the fireplace and started building a fire. "We'll need this in a bit to knock the chill off."

After the fire had a good start, Michael pulled some fresh trout from the fridge. I picked a bottle of white wine from the fridge. I opened the bottle and poured two glasses while Michael started preparing the trout. We dined on sautéed trout with green onions and rice.

After we did a quick clean up in the kitchen, we took the bottle of wine and settled in on the sofa. Michael had turned on the CD player with some soft jazz. My mind slipped back to a few days ago when Michael had picked me up at the airport.

I had flown from Richmond to Salt Lake City, making a connection to Great Falls. I was a nervous wreck when we touched down in Salt Lake. Not because of the flight, it was smooth as silk the whole way. It was my nerves, stressing on my decision to fly almost all the way across the country to spend ten days with a man I only knew by emails and phone conversations. I had promised to call Michael when I arrived, but I found a bar instead. After I downed a tall glass of beer, I got the nerve to call.

"Hey Michael." I was trying not to let him know just how nervous I was, trying to sound like I had so many other times when I had called him.

"Hello! So you didn't back out after all?" He laughed.

"Nope. I'm in Salt Lake. My flight is leaving on time. You still going to pick me up?" Damn, I shouldn't have said that. That doesn't show any self-confidence, I thought almost out loud.

"Of course. It has taken too much persuading on my end to get you here. I will be there and I promise to be on time."

"Okay, see you in four hours." And I ended the call. Four hours. I needed another beer, but decided I better not show up under the influence. I had several hours to kill, so I shopped and drank coffee. The flight to Great Falls was a little under two hours.

My flight to Great Falls was uneventful. I enjoyed the clear skies and the beauty of the mountains below. My stomach was in knots as the plane touched down and we taxied to the gate. I was laughing to myself. Great Falls was listed as an International Airport, all four gates. As soon as the plane stopped at the gate, people started rising and retrieving their overhead baggage. I sat still. When most of the people in front of me had left the plane, I stood and started for the door. I could feel my knees shaking.

This was crazy. I was too old to be acting like a school girl on her first car date. This had been months in the planning. I made my way up the hallway and out through the security doors. My eyes were scanning the faces of people waiting for their friends or loved ones. There to the back of the group of people, I could see the top of a man's

54

*head. Just as I was thinking that must be Michael,
the people in front of him parted and I got a full
view. It was him.*

*He was standing there smiling. Holy crap,
he's better looking than his photo. I couldn't help
but smile. He stood there, all six foot four inches of
him, long and lean. A tall drink of water as Joan
and Patty would have said years ago. He wore a
green short sleeved shirt, tucked into the waist of
his blue jeans. He had on hiking boots which made
him even taller. He was holding a bouquet of
flowers. White daisies, they were perfect.*

*I made my way to him, he handed me the
daisies and bent down and kissed me on the cheek.
"Welcome to Montana."*

"Thank you. These are lovely."

*"Not as lovely as you," he said just loud
enough that I could hear him.*

*When I looked up, he was still smiling. It
made me feel that he wasn't disappointed in what
he saw.*

"Hey, where are you?" Michael asked as he
took my wine glass and poured us both a bit more,
emptying the bottle.

"Oh, I was thinking about my flight out here
and you meeting me at the airport."

"That's funny, I was thinking about that
earlier."

"Really?"

"Yes; I was thinking just how beautiful you are, even with the new haircut."

"Oh God, you had to remind me! I started to laugh, as it was all I could do. Crying wouldn't make my chopped up hair grow any faster.

Michael leaned over toward me. "Can I kiss you?"

"Yes, as soon as I get a shower. I'll be fast, I promise." I jumped up and trotted to the bathroom. I took a quick shower, threw on some fresh clothes, and returned to the sofa in record time. I took a seat in the same spot I had left only minutes ago.

"Okay, I'll try this again: can I kiss you?" Michael asked with a soft smile.

It was right then and there I knew I was going to give in to him. The day had been perfect. I might as well give it a try and see if the night could be perfect also. Instead of answering him, I turned toward him and kissed him. I made the first move and allowed my lips to part just enough that he knew I was inviting his tongue to explore.

He accepted the invitation and slowly ran his tongue over my bottom lip. After a long warm kiss, I broke away to set my wine glass on the table. Michael did the same. We both gave a little laugh and then he laid me backward on the sofa. There was no tension in my body, just anticipation.

Michael lay on his side, facing me, his face in the crook of my neck. I could feel his warm steady breath. Each breath sent tingling waves of pleasure through my body. He nibbled at my ear and then he turned my face toward his with gentle fingers on my chin. He kissed me softly at first. Each kiss grew more intense and so was the electricity between us. People talk about having sparks fly when they are with someone very special, and now I knew what they were trying to explain.

In one smooth movement, Michael was lying flat on the sofa and he had me on top of him. I was sitting on top of his lap, well aware of his erection. There was no way a woman wouldn't notice him. I wasn't sure if I was ready for what was waiting there for me.

Michael tugged at my shirt, lifting it up and over my head. He smiled at me when he noticed my white lacy bra that hooked in the front. "Do you mind?" he asked as he unhooked the closure.

"No," I hissed as I sucked in a breath.

He reached up and pushed the straps off over my shoulders, allowing my bra to fall away. "My God, you are beautiful." He sat up and slid back toward the arm of the sofa, holding me to his lap. Then starting at my neck he moved his warm, wet tongue down to my breast. I could feel my nipples harden with excitement. I held the back of his head to keep him there, nibbling at my breast, first one and then the other.

"I want you naked and in bed," he said as he broke away from my grip.

"Naked, yes," I said as I stood up. My jeans slipped off easily as I was bare footed after my shower. I stood there in my white lace panties, feeling sexy for the first time in a very long time. I hooked my thumbs at my hips and slowly wiggled them down to the floor. I took Michael by the hands and pulled him up from the sofa. As he stood in front of me, I unhooked his belt, unbuttoned his jeans, and got the fly open. I didn't waste any time, and I got his jeans and boxers off in one move.

I was not sure where all the daring actions were coming from, but I took his erection in my hand and led him to the end of the sofa. I took a seat on the tall arm and pulled him toward me. Without any words between us, Michael guided himself slowly into me. I wrapped my legs around him and pulled him as deep as I could into me.

He started to back away just a bit, but I held tight. "Please don't move for just a minute. I just want to feel you inside of me for a bit."

"I'll do my best," he whispered as he started kissing my neck.

I held him there for as long as my body would stand it. Not having sex in more months than I wanted to even remember, my body was ready to explode. As I felt my excitement growing from within and a trembling growing in my legs, I unwound my legs and pushed Michael away from me.

"Oh, I thought you were about to…"

"I was, but I don't want to climax just yet. This is just too good."

"You can if you want. I will wait until next time." He smiled at me as he stepped back toward me. Again he guided himself ever so gently into me; then pulled my legs up and around him again. He didn't stroke me like most men would have, instead he grabbed my backside and pulled me to him while he pushed deeper.

I was right; this was too good. I held onto him with hands and legs as I felt my body grow with heated excitement. I could feel the pulsating thump start deep within me until my whole body was keeping rhythm with my pleasure, exploding around him deep inside of me.

He never made an attempt to move until he was sure I was complete. I felt light headed as he pulled out of me. I opened my eyes, finding him standing before me, his green eyes almost glowing and the rest of him standing at attention. He stepped over to the table, grabbed a glass and took a large drink. I took one, too. Before I could put the glass back on the table, Michael pulled me into the bedroom.

He fell onto the bed, lying on his back, and motioned for me to join him. I took another drink of wine, set the glass on the nightstand, and slid onto the bed next to him. "Close your eyes," he whispered.

I closed my eyes and seconds later I felt something soft running down my body, starting at the tip of my nose, down my chin, continuing down the middle of my body, over one hip, down that leg then making its way up the other leg. I couldn't stand it any longer; I had to open my eyes.

"Tisk, tisk, tisk, you're peeking." Michael chuckled.

I saw that he had a Peacock feather in his hand, allowing it to run softly over my body. I closed my eyes again and enjoyed the tingling sensations that were running up and down my naked body. I wanted to ask where the feather had come from, but I really didn't care.

"Control your breathing, slow and easy," he whispered into my ear. "Easy." His voice was deep but smooth like velvet.

I did as I was told. Slowing my breath, relaxing my body, trying to only think of the feather moving across my skin. Slowly I relaxed my muscles one by one just like in Yoga class. I was practically floating above the bed. I had no idea how long I had been in this relaxed state of being when the feather stopped just below my navel.

"Easy, breathe slow and deep." The words were bouncing off my stomach, his warm breath caressing my skin. Then I felt his hands under my knees as he lifted and separated my legs. "Easy, don't move. Promise?"

I couldn't even answer. With bated breath, I waited for the next sensation. I felt the feather moving slowly from my navel toward my leg, only this time making a circular motion around the center of my body. Touching the skin in the crease of my legs was driving me crazy with desire. The only word that escaped my lips was, "Please!"

"Please?" he asked and then in one swift movement, I felt his tongue invade my most private part.

Just as I was about to climax again, he left me. I opened my eyes to see him on his knees between my legs. I took him in my hand and guided him into me. That was all it took, as in less than a minute we both were spent. Soaked with sweat, we both looked like someone had poured a pitcher of water on us.

"One time my mother told me, the older we get the better the sex gets. I always thought she was making that stuff up. You just made a believer," I managed to whisper.

"Your mother was a smart lady." Michael handed me a glass of wine. We finished our glasses of wine before we fell asleep. I do remember the quilt being pulled up over our bodies as the night air crept into the cabin.

9

Virginia

Five thirty in the morning and I had already hit the snooze button three times. I really had to get up and ready for work. Instead, I lay in my bed thinking about the conversation the night before with a stranger on the Internet. We had been communicating on the website every night for almost a week.

Since I had moved to Richmond, I had a regular routine. Awake at five, taking thirty minutes to do some kind of exercise, either walking or on my fold-up home gym. Shower by five thirty, dressed, small breakfast, check emails, and out the door by seven fifteen. Evenings were filled with a regular routine as well. Depending on traffic, I would make it home between six and seven. Although one night because of a horrible accident it was after eight before I pulled into my parking place.

In the evenings, I would change clothes and walk or ride my bicycle around the area known as The Fan. I loved this part of Richmond. I was told it was called The Fan because all the streets fanned out from the most eastern part of the city. The development of this part of the city dated earlier than the Civil War. Many of the homes were lost during the fires in the war. The homes and buildings that were left had been restored to their grandeur. Many of the homes were kept with furniture from the period in the downstairs parlors. People would leave the drapes open in the evenings, allowing passersby a view. Most of the homes had modern kitchens and living quarters. Since the University of Virginia was only a few blocks from my apartment, there were always people on the streets, walking or riding their bikes.

After my exercising in the evenings, I would do any apartment cleaning that needed done, have a little dinner of sorts, then settle in with a book or watch some television. I tried to keep busy so my mind wouldn't return to Alabama, back to the bad memories of a marriage gone wrong.

I wasn't sure, but I thought I still loved John. After all, we had been together for almost fifteen years. So many good times drowned out by bad things. So many unanswered questions. Had we grown apart or had he just lost interest in me? Maybe it was our jobs.

John was a city police officer when we met. It was as they say, love at first sight. We had gone out once for coffee and then it was game on. Within two months we were living together. Four years after that we married. I'm still not sure why we married other than it was the thing to do at the time. We were happy living together. Wasn't marriage just a piece of paper?

Both of our jobs were demanding. John worked long hours as an undercover cop. Because of my banking background, I was working for an oil company operating a small chain of convenience stores. Both of us found ourselves on call twenty four hours a day, seven days a week. No routines for us and barely time to see each other much less have time off to enjoy life.

This past week had been completely different. I was still trying to decide if it was a good thing. I had a steady date at eight every night. I found myself rushing home so that I had time to keep my regular routine and still be able to get online at eight.

The second night of my on-line dating, I started making notes as we communicated. At first I thought making notes would make me out as a stalker. Then I convinced myself I was just protecting my feelings. I had too many lies in my past to really trust anyone again. Patty had told me years ago at breakfast that I was too trusting.

We had just sat down at our favorite booth at the Big Boys one Saturday morning. Coffee was ordered and all three of us looked like we had been rode hard and put up wet. Patty and Joan were hung over; I was just sleep deprived.

"Next time I leave you girls to go meet a guy, tell me no." I took a long drag on my half smoked cigarette.

"What happened?" Joan asked as she stole a cigarette from my pack.

"I met Dan again last night. He's so handsome, how could I resist? When I left the bar I met him at the Holiday Inn. I know, I know. But why not? We have been talking almost every night since we met. We're footloose and fancy free."

"Why am I thinking this isn't going to end well?" Patty frowned.

"Because it doesn't! We went down to the bar at the Inn, had a few drinks, and danced until the band quit at one thirty. I didn't know it, but Dan had got us a room. It was a surprise."

"Okay, that sounds like a good night." Joan smirked.

"We got to the room; he unlocked the door and carried me into the room. There were roses and wine waiting for us. How damn romantic is that?"

"Details, girl, details!" Patty coaxed me.

"We drank the wine and slowly undressed each other. I don't think you need any more details." I was laughing.

"What the hell happened?" Joan was getting anxious.

"I was down to my bra and panties. Dan was naked, all of him! Things were getting hot and heavy when there was a knock at the door. I freaked out! Dan put his finger to his lips, making the sign for me to be quiet. But the knocking got louder. Dan pulled his jeans on, went to the door, and there stood a pissed off blonde with a baseball bat. She tried to push past him, but he stopped her and shooed her back outside. I went to the window just in time to see her bust the windshield of his Mustang."

"Jesus, Dawn. You can pick em." Joan shook her head.

"Yeah, they ended up leaving. I got dressed and went home. It must have been his wife, even though he told me they were divorced, or separated, or not living together." I was holding back some tears.

"Geez, Dawn, how long have you known Dan?" Patty asked as the waitress poured us all some coffee.

"Three weeks? Maybe longer. I can't remember. When did we all go to Jackson on that road trip?"

"Three weeks ago," Joan popped off. "That's when I met Bill."

"How was I supposed to know he was lying to me?" I felt myself getting defensive, but Patty had a point.

"So did you ask?" Patty lit a cigarette and blew the smoke toward me.

"I think so, maybe." Now I was feeling really naive.

"You trust everyone," Patty said quietly.

"Maybe you should take notes!" Patty laughed.

"I do."

Patty and I both looked at her in disbelief. "Really?"

"Well, not really notes, but I keep a journal. You would be surprised how many lies I catch people in by going back over my diary. Not just men but people at work, too. I have kept a diary since high school," Joan said with a big smile.

"Are we in your diary?" Patty asked.

"Of course!" Joan gave us a devilish smile.

From time to time for several years after that conversation, I would write in a journal. Mostly silly stuff, or so I thought at the time. Sometimes I would go back and read about weekends all of us girls had too much fun and yet there were other times we all were in tears.

I hadn't kept a journal in years. My marriage to John had become too sad to record on paper. This new on-line relationship was different; it was safe, I kept telling myself. I found an old notebook just before eight. I laid it and an ink pen next to my laptop. Just as I sat down my computer pinged. I felt a smile turn the corners of my lips upward.

"Good evening," the popup conversation screen read.

"Back at ya," I typed.

"Say, this typing is getting old. Can I have your phone number? I would much rather talk to you."

I sat there drawing circles on the paper, reading what few notes I had taken the last couple of days. I hadn't written much, too busy typing. I could hear Cindy's words telling me to get his phone number. She had also told me to Google him, but I hadn't done that either. Was I being naïve again? *What can it hurt?* I asked myself. *He's in Montana, I'm in Virginia. Go for it.* I slowly typed my cell phone number, and I took a deep breath as I hit the enter key.

I wrote in the notebook the date and that I had sent Michael my phone number. Before I could put the pen down, my cell phone rang. I picked it up to see a phone number with a 406 area code.

"Hello?" I tried not to sound excited.

A deep smooth masculine voice asked, "Dawn?"

"Yes, this is she." I sounded like a telemarketer had just called.

"So, you did give me the right phone number?" He chuckled.

"Why wouldn't I?" I found myself laughing also.

"You have a lovely laugh. It's good to finally talk to you. My fingers were getting tired."

"I key all day long at work, so I have to agree with you." I was trying to sound casual and confident.

"The photo on your profile, how long ago was that taken? You sure are easy on the eyes."

"I took that of myself a few weeks ago. I was dressed for a dinner at a friend's home."

"Not a date?" he asked.

"No, not a date! I haven't dated since my divorce," I said firmly.

"Really? I would think men would be beating your door down. I would be knocking if I lived near you."

"That's very nice of you, but I'm not ready to answer the knocks on the door." I was laughing again.

Michael kept me laughing. I looked at the clock and it was almost midnight. "Michael, I need to get off the phone. It's almost midnight and I need to get up at five."

"Holy crap, I didn't realize we had been on the phone that long. I'm sorry. Goodnight. Talk to you tomorrow."

"Goodnight."

It was then I took a look at my notes I had been scribbling. Most of the information was repeated from our on-line conversations.

Gunsmith.

Divorced.

One grown daughter.

Works at home.

Builds his own guns and knives.

Has a shop on property.

Likes hunting, fishing, dogs, guns, his cabin in the woods, hiking.

Doesn't date.

I had written that he doesn't date. Maybe I misunderstood him. Why would a man be on an on-line dating site if he "doesn't date?" That didn't make sense. I should have asked him why, but I couldn't remember why the subject was dropped.

I jumped up from the sofa, brushed my teeth, turned out the lights, and checked the clock to make sure the alarm was set. I was in bed trying to recall the conversation when it came to me.

"You wouldn't answer the door if I came knocking?" he asked.

"Oh, a date?"

"I don't date.

"Me either." And we both laughed, but he never explained why he didn't date.

10

Alabama

The alarm clock came to life, but instead of hitting the snooze button I shut it completely off. The bed was warm and so was the breeze coming through the window next to the bed. I really didn't want to drag myself out of my cozy spot.

Again, I found myself alone in the king size bed. This was happening more often than any wife would want. John had been working on a drug task force for several months. During that time we had hardly seen one another. When we did, it was in passing. I would be going to work and he would be coming in from another stakeout or drug buy. I wouldn't say we were getting along, but we weren't fighting either. We didn't see each other enough to fight.

I had just climbed out of the shower and was getting myself together when I heard the door to the basement garage open. "John, is that you?"

"Yeah! You still home?"

"That's a silly question. I couldn't ask if that's you if I wasn't home." I was trying to be funny, but John wasn't in a funny mood.

"You always have to be a smart ass?" I heard him rummaging through the frig looking for something to eat.

"You hungry? I can fix you something."

"Naw, you better get to work. I'll fix something."

As I was getting dressed, John was running the shower as hard as the water pressure would allow. A relaxing method of his after a stressful night. His cell phone was dancing across the wooden kitchen table. Before I could pick it up and take it to him, whoever was calling had hung up. Shortly afterward the landline rang.

"Hello?" I answered.

"Oh, is John there?" asked a woman.

"He's in the shower. Can I ask who's calling?"

"Just tell him Trista called." The line went dead.

Trista was a dispatcher that had been fired from the police department several weeks before for causing a lot of trouble for several officers. She was single and wanted to be married to a cop, no matter what she had to do or who she had to hurt. She was already the cause of two marriage breakups.

I walked into the bathroom through a cloud of steam and knocked on the glass shower door. John cracked it open. "What?"

"Trista just called. Said to tell you she called." I would never forget the deer in the headlights look John gave me that morning. Maybe it was a hand caught in the cookie jar look and Trista was the cookie jar.

Trying to be nonchalant, John pulled the shower door closed and gave me an, "Okay."

I left for work and I assumed John would be getting some sleep as he was working again that night. When I arrived home that evening, instead of pulling my car up under the carport, I pulled into the lower driveway and parked in front of the garage door next to John's undercover car. As I got out of my car, I noticed an envelope under the driver's side windshield wiper of John's car.

I pulled the envelope out from under the wiper to see it was a greeting card with John written on the front in very feminine style handwriting. I opened the envelope to find a thank you card. Simple and sweet. The cover just stated thank you. I opened the card to see, **Thank you for a wonderful night. T.**

My fears that had been building up because of the rumors coming from the police department flooded over me. Tears started running down my cheeks. I stuffed the card back into its envelope, turned, and made my way into the house. John was standing at the kitchen counter making a cup of coffee. He looked like he had just got out of bed.

"What's wrong? Why are you crying?" he asked as he tried to grab my shoulders.

I backed away, handing him the envelope. "What's this?"

"Well hell, how would I know? I just got up."

I threw the envelope down on the counter and walked away. As I sat on the sofa in the living room, I heard John let out a long sigh. Then I heard the garbage can lid open and shut.

"I can explain," he said, standing in the doorway.

"I'm not sure if I want an explanation. Did you work last night?" I was doing my best to stay calm and stop crying.

"Yes," he said quietly, but he wouldn't even look me in the eyes. Staring at the floor, he whispered, "Yes, but not all night."

You trust everyone, Patty's words haunted me, as always.

"Where were you the rest of the night?" I wasn't sure if I wanted the truth.

"I was up at Denny's having coffee with Trista."

"Oh, is that why you were in such a mood this morning? If so, maybe you should hang out with someone else? Like maybe your wife?"

"It wasn't like that. She was at the station when I got off stakeout and she needed someone to talk to. She's really not a bad person." He was still looking at the floor.

"So there aren't any single men for her to talk to about her problems? Seems all her problems extend from her relationships with married men. I do hear things, you know."

"Maybe you shouldn't believe all you hear?" John was now sounding irritated.

"Does that include what I hear from you?" I probably shouldn't have said that, but it was how I

74

was feeling. My heart was breaking and I wanted to strike back.

"Fuck you! I wouldn't be able to say anything right at this point. I'll talk to you later. I'm going to work!" With that, John changed clothes, grabbed his gear, and left.

Later when I was cleaning up the kitchen, I opened the lid on the garbage can. The card and envelope were gone. Maybe I had just thought I heard the lid open earlier. I could only think that John had kept the card from Trista.

The next morning I called my boss and asked for a few days off. I packed a bag and left a note for John.

John, I'm going down to Gulf Shores for a few days. I'll be back on Sunday. If you need me, I have my cell phone with me. D

I spent the five hour drive trying to decide what I needed to do. I still loved John, but his job had come between us. Now Trista was doing her best to come between us as well. I had to be honest with myself. If John was totally happy, he would not let Trista creep into our life, driving a wedge between us. He had to have known how much this would hurt me.

When I arrived in Gulf Shores and found the motel, there was a message from Donna that she had to work and wouldn't be joining me after all. She would call me tomorrow. Great, I thought as I finished checking into my room. I wasn't going to waste three days off from work. I changed into my swimsuit and a t-shirt. I grabbed a beer from my cooler and walked out onto the deck overlooking the pure white sands of Gulf Shores.

I flopped down on a lounge chair, sucked my cold beer down, and let the warm ocean breeze kiss my skin. I tried not to think of how much better this would be if John was here with me. Then I realized he was probably spending this free time from me with Trista because she had so many problems. Three beers later, I couldn't have given a flip about John or Trista.

Three more beers and the sun had sunk into the gulf, leaving behind bold pink and purple clouds. It was early, but I had too many beers. I found my way into the room, turned on the TV, flopped into bed, and allowed myself to drift away. My heart wasn't hurting if I was sleeping.

***

I was hurting the next morning when I woke up. I was still in my swimsuit and t-shirt. My head felt like someone had smacked me with a hammer during the night. I showered and got dressed. I began checking my cell phone for any missed calls, but there was nothing.

I made my way across the side street to a little café for some coffee and toast. After several cups, I was feeling better. I tried to convince myself not to call home, but I did. There was no answer, just the answering machine picking up, which made me feel even more empty and hurt.

Saturday was a repeat of Friday. Beer, patio, lounge chair, and sunset. The only difference was I stayed awake long enough to switch from beer to rum. I know better, but it seemed like the right thing to do at the time.

Sunday morning found me on the short sofa in the room. I hadn't even made it to the bed the night before. The TV was blaring an infomercial of some kind. I hit the off button and stood, begging the great god of drunks to make my head stop hurting. My prayer was not answered.

I looked in the bathroom mirror and did not like what I saw. "Geez, Dawn, you aren't twenty five any more. Get your shit together," I whispered to myself. I would have yelled, but my head was pounding too hard.

I stood in the shower allowing the hot water to nurse me back to feeling partly human. I decided I might as well pack my things and head home. No sense in dragging this out any longer. I made it home in less than four hours.

I really had no idea what I was going to say or do for that matter. Deep down inside, I was hoping John had decided I was what he wanted and we would work things out. But as always I knew life did not have a fairy tale ending.

Pulling up into the upper driveway, I had seen John's undercover car parked across the street. I left my bag in the car and unlocked the side door. After listening for any sounds of life before I walked all the way into the mudroom, I set my purse on the table by the door. "John?" I yelled.

"In here," came his voice from the living room.

"Hey," I said as I walked through the kitchen. I wasn't surprised when I saw that he was packing some things into some boxes. Like a fool, I asked, "What are you doing?"

"Packing up my things. I'm moving out."

"So, this is how it ends?" I already knew the answer.

"I just don't think I want to be married anymore. It's best if I leave."

I could feel the air leaving my lungs, taking my heart with it. "Jesus, John, you think you would have made up your mind about that before you asked me to marry you. You picked a fine time to decide this now."

"I don't want to hurt you anymore than I already have and if I stay it will only get worse. It's me, not you."

My mind raced with those words. I had heard them before. Empty words when someone is breaking off a relationship. I wondered if those words were supposed to make the hurt lessen.

I couldn't even answer or I didn't have an answer. My heart was broken, again. I swore to myself that this would be the last time. I watched as John packed his things and loaded them into his car. Before he could come back into the house to say goodbye I locked myself in the bathroom. I stayed there until I heard his car drive off.

I wanted to cry. Maybe throw something, breaking something into tiny pieces to match the broken pieces of my heart. I had fallen for John heart and soul. It would take more than this to break the bonds I felt for him.

I unpacked my bag and made myself some ice tea. I sat on the front porch drinking my tea and watching the sun set behind the tall pines in the park across from our home. I felt like Scarlet O'Hara. I would think about this tomorrow. Tonight I had to get my things ready for Monday and a new work day.

***

The days turned into a week. Every night I would pray that I would hear from John, but no call came. I refused to give in and call him. The weeks turned into a month and still no word. Several of my friends said they saw him back in uniform and working patrol. Of course I took a double take every time I saw a police car, but it was never him.

The second month he was gone, I came home from work and there was a note waiting for me on the kitchen table.

D,

I just wanted you to know that I picked up the rest of my things, including all of my guns. I also hired Bob Taylor to take care of the divorce. We both know that I am not what you need. You know my background. You know I tried. You should have someone that can give you the love you deserve. In my own way, I will always love you but it's best for all concerned that we end things. You should be getting papers served in a few days. I hope you will agree with what I had written up.

J

I sat at the table staring at the note. All hope left my heart. I could not hurt any more than I was right at that moment.

Just like he said, two days later there was a knock at my office door. A County Sheriff walked in and asked my name. I repeated my full name and he handed me an envelope. "Consider yourself served." He turned and left. The envelope was from R. Taylor, Attorney at Law. I picked up the envelope, tucked it in my brief case, locked up the office, and headed for home.

I sat in my chair in the living room with a bottle of beer trying to get the nerve to open the envelope. After my second beer, I finally tore the packet open. I started reading.

Irreconcilable differences. *So that's what this is*, I thought to myself. Kind of hard to reconcile when you haven't talked to each other for two months. I read the list of shared property. He was leaving me everything except the things he now had with him, which was his clothes and the guns he owned before we met. I wondered if that was because he was feeling so guilty or because he didn't want me to struggle to start over. I was guessing by the time I finished my third beer that it really wouldn't matter.

I dug out a pen from my purse and signed the papers. There, over and done. I stuffed the papers into a supplied return envelope and sealed the flap shut. The instructions stated if both parties agreed, with no contest, if I didn't hire my own attorney, the divorce would be final in three months.

I walked into the bathroom, started the hot water running, stripped and stepped into the filling tub. I wanted another beer, but decided against it as I let the hot water wash the hurt away. I soaked in the tub until I was all wrinkled and the water was cold. After I dried and put on a clean night gown, I looked at my left hand. The gold band stared back at me. I took it off and placed it in the jewelry box that John bought for me a few years back. *I'll think about it tomorrow*, I thought as I lay in the empty bed, pulling the quilt up to my chin.

Three months later, we were divorced.

11

Montana

Waking up with bright sunlight streaking through the windows, I opened my eyes to find myself alone in the bed. I was in no big hurry to get up. The room was chilly and I was snuggled under a warm quilt. I laid there listening for any signs of life in the cabin. Nothing but quiet and a few birds chirping in the pines. There was a slight breeze as I could hear the pine needles whispering. I was absolutely relaxed and calm. I haven't felt this way in a long time. The question I kept asking myself was: was it the company of the man I had shared the night with or this peaceful place in the mountains? The longer I was here, the more I didn't want to leave. Richmond seemed a million miles away. Even in the middle of Sunday night when Richmond was really at rest, it was never this quiet.

I finally couldn't stay in bed any longer. Making my morning trip to the bathroom, I could smell the remnants of Michael's shower, manly and clean. I felt myself smile as I remembered last night.

I put on an oversized flannel shirt and ventured to the kitchen. There on the counter I found a note.

Dawn, good morning. I have run to town to pick up Jake from the vets and a few things from the grocery store. Will be home in a few hours. M

At first I was angry that he would go to town and leave me here all alone. I wanted to get my hair trimmed up from my whack job. No vehicle, no real idea where I was, no neighbors, no cell phone, and no gun. The only thing between me and something bad happening was a locked door and windows with bars. I didn't even know how long he had been gone. What if something happened to him? I didn't have a cell phone signal out here. No one knew where I was, except for Michael. "Hell, you don't even know where you are, dumb ass!"

Okay, stop thinking like this, I told myself. *Get a freaking grip.* Coffee, I needed some coffee. I made a pot and waited patiently for it to brew. Finally, I was able to pour a cup. With the first sip, I felt myself calming down.

I opened the front door, stepped out onto the porch, and took a seat in one of the rockers. I pulled my knees up to my chest and let the sun shine on me, warming me to the core. If I lived in Augusta, I would be spending every minute I could up here. What a beautiful place. My mind slipping back to my arrival, but I still couldn't remember the ride here.

We walked down to the baggage claim area to retrieve my luggage. We were making small talk about my flight across the country. After my luggage finally made its way onto the carrousel, Michael grabbed both bags and pulled them out to his truck.

He tossed my bags into the back of the truck; an older model four by four, Ford F-150. "Does everyone in Montana have a four by four?" I asked.

"If they have any sense they do." He laughed. "Have to remember in this part of Montana it may be seventy-five degrees in the morning and snowing by dark."

I climbed up into the cab. The truck was dark green and had a tan interior. "Wow, do you ever drive this? It looks brand new."

"I cleaned it up for my company. Trust me, this doesn't happen too often." He laughed.

"Now that's the way to make a girl feel special. Pick her up in a clean truck!" I was smiling and feeling a bit more at ease.

"Are you hungry?" Michael asked as he started the truck and slipped it into gear.

"A little, but I can wait a while."

"So would you like the two dollar tour or the five dollar tour?"

"What's the difference?"

"Three dollars." He was laughing, but then explained. "It's the difference between seeing most of town or just the special places. We have plenty of time for the five dollar tour before we head to Augusta."

"Okay, five dollar tour it is. We can eat later." I settled into the seat, buckling my seat belt.

As we left the airport parking lot, we pulled up into a park that over looked the city. The airport was on a high ridge that over looked the Missouri River that snaked its way around and through the city. I found myself wondering how Lewis and Clark might have seen this so long ago.

"Wow, that's beautiful. I bet it's really pretty at night."

"Yep; just like looking at Las Vegas, only smaller." Now we both were laughing.

From the top of the airport hill into town there was just one road, Interstate 15. No frontage road on that part of the interstate. We exited the interstate, taking the main road into the sprawling city. Great Falls had a lot of history that I had studied before my flight. I didn't want to be taken completely by surprise. We drove along the river, from one end of town to the other. Then we made our way out to the Black Eagle dam. Again, I wondered how the falls might have looked to the Natives or the first white people, long before the dam was built. I had seen a few photos when I was researching.

"This hillside is where the old smelter once stood. All those stone blocks you see are the leftovers from the old foundations," Michael explained.

"I like having my own private tour guide."

We spent several hours walking along the river at several different parks. Then we drove downtown. Great Falls downtown area was suffering just like most downtown areas across the country. I could tell by the beautiful empty buildings that downtown was once the hub of activity for the city. "It's a shame that cities lose these beautiful buildings to malls and strip malls." I pointed to a five story brick building that was now some sort of *business. "Was that a department store at one time?"*

"Yep, it went out of business when the mall opened up out on the now main road to the south of here. They redirected traffic to that road and downtown dried up."

"Downtown Richmond looks the same, only bigger."

"You wouldn't believe it, but during the fifties and sixties Great Falls was really a hot spot for entertainers. Why even the King himself performed here. J.F.K. came once, too, before the Cuban Missile Crisis." Michael stopped and smiled at me. "We should be thinking about heading to Augusta. We can stop on the way and get a bite to eat, if that's alright with you."

"You're the tour guide." My nerves had calmed down some and I was feeling more relaxed being with this man I only knew from texting and phone calls.

I pushed the last words out of my mind that Cindy had said to me before I left. "Dawn, are you sure you want to do this? Be careful."

As I sat on the front porch in the warm sunlight, I started to wonder how safe I really was way out here in the wilds of Montana. Since I didn't know what time Michael would be back, I decided to get a bath and at least look human when he did return.

I locked the front door, grabbed another cup of coffee, and headed to the bathroom. I pondered the idea of taking a shower. If I got in the shower I

86

would not be able to hear anything else going on in or around the cabin. I laughed at myself. "Geez, a little paranoid, aren't you?" Only no one answered. I decided a shower would be fine. Finally convincing myself that I would be safer out here than I was in the shower in my little apartment in Richmond, I headed to the bathroom. Just how much crime could there be way out here?

I stayed in the lovely hot shower until the water started cooling off. The hot water tank didn't like my kind of long showers. I threw on clean clothes and dried my hair with a towel. I applied a little blush and some mascara, adding just a little color to my pale complexion. Looking at myself in the mirror, I whispered, "Okay, Michael, you can come back anytime."

I grabbed my coffee cup, warmed it up a bit with some more coffee, and returned back to the porch. The sun was still warming the rocker so I flopped back down. After finishing the coffee, I was thinking about taking a little walk around the cabin when I heard something moving through the woods. Maybe a deer. I was thinking it was moving too fast to be a bear. Maybe an elk, as we were in elk country. I stood and was scanning as deep as I could see into the forest.

All of a sudden, a big black Labrador came bounding out of the trees. "Jake!"

He stopped, looked at me, and started wagging his tail. He came at me in a full out run and it looked like he was smiling.

"Hey," Michael sounded as he broke the tree line.

"About time you got back. I was feeling lonely," I half shouted back as I rubbed Jake.

Michael had a large backpack strapped to his back and was carrying another large duffel. He laid them both on the porch deck then stepped up next to me.

"Good morning,"

"Good afternoon."

"I didn't have the heart to wake you this morning. I woke up before daylight and decided to go to town and pick up Jake and a few supplies. You're not mad, are you?"

"No, I guess not. I did feel rather abandoned when I first realized you left me here. I don't exactly know my way around here, you know?"

"Well, I see a bear didn't drag you off while I was gone."

"That's not the point. What if something had happened to you?"

"Okay, I get it. It won't happen again!" He grabbed the backpack and duffel and pushed past me into the cabin.

Following him and Jake into the cabin, I sat down at the bar. "Hey, I didn't mean to piss you off. I was just trying to explain how I felt."

"I said, I get it. Drop it, okay?"

I sat and watched as he unpacked the supplies. I was thinking there was more than enough to keep us supplied for weeks. I was only supposed to stay ten days or so. "Wow, are we having company?"

"Company?"

"Well, yeah, look at all you brought. That's a lot of stuff."

"No company comes here unless I bring them and I haven't invited anyone up here but you in a long time."

I sat there trying to remember our conversations regarding the cabin, and he was right. I didn't remember him telling me much about visitors to his secret place.

12

Virginia

"Cindy, I just don't know what to think of this guy. We spent the evening on the phone again." Cindy was pouring me a cup of coffee. I had driven over to her place before we went out for a girl's day of shopping. Ted was up in D.C. again, working the weekend.

"He seems nice from what you told me. Has he said anything creepy?"

"No, not really. Maybe it's just that I don't have that much confidence in men being what they say they are."

"You said you were taking notes. Have you noticed anything that doesn't click?" She sat down beside me.

"You know I felt creepy taking notes so I stopped. But what I do have is nothing that sounds off any alarms. He talks about his daughter and ex with kindness. He does seem to spend a lot of time alone. But then so do I."

"Not lately. You have been spending time with him on the phone when you're not at work." She laughed.

"The other night he told me about his cabin he has up in the mountains west of where he lives. He said it's a stretch to get to, but it's well worth the hike. Said he has to hike in from a trail head. Sounds like it's his get away from everything place, a hunting cabin until the snow gets too deep. I wouldn't mind having a place like that."

"You and me both. That doesn't sound creepy. Maybe he's a Unabomber or axe murderer and that's where he does his dirty deeds!"

"That's not funny! But then, that has crossed my mind."

"Did you Google him?"

"Yes. I found a couple of things on him. He's a well-known gunsmith and gun expert. Has written several articles about guns. He told me that before I Googled him. He likes guns, so I guess he wouldn't be axing women!"

"So his story checks out. Maybe he's on the up and up."

"Yeah, so was John Collins."

"Who?"

"Never mind, long story."

Cindy and I had a fun day shopping and having a late lunch at our favorite bistro. I dropped her off and headed home. Just as I was pulling up into the parking lot my cell phone rang. I figured Cindy had forgotten something in the car and I answered without looking at the screen.

"What did you forget?"

"Dawn?"

My heart stopped in my chest. Anger flew all over me. How could just the sound of his voice throw me for a loop after all this time? I wanted to hang up. No, I wanted to throw the phone out the window. I hated myself for feeling this way.

"Just a second, I'm parking the car." I could hardly breathe as I shoved the car into park. "What do you want, John?"

"I want to talk to you. You have a few minutes?"

"About what? I think we have said it all. Aren't you happily divorced; footloose and fancy free?"

"No. Please, can we just talk?"

"I'm just pulling up into the parking lot. I have some things I need to get into the house. Call me back in ten."

"Okay." And the line went dead.

I sat there for a few minutes trying to calm down. "Okay, Dawn, get your act together. Get your packages and get in the apartment." *I'm getting really good at this talking to myself,* I thought.

I sat at the little table, looking at the cell phone, willing it not to ring. The screen lit up, regardless of my willing. An Alabama phone number appeared. "Damn!"

I flipped the phone open. "What?"

"It's John. You have a few minutes now?"

"A few. What's up?"

"I'm on my way to Virginia. Dad is back in the hospital. I didn't know if you knew or not."

"Nope, no one has called. How bad?"

"Not good."

"Tomorrow is Sunday. I will go and see him. I'm sorry. The cancer is back?"

"I guess it really never left. I just wanted you to know that he was back at the V.A. and I was coming to town."

"Nice of you to give me a notice."

"Maybe we could have dinner?"

"I don't think that would be a good idea."

"You found someone else?"

"No, not really."

Before he could ask me any other questions, my phoned beeped. I looked at the screen and it was Michael calling. The first thing that ran through my mind was I was saved.

"John, I have another call coming in, I need to go." Before he could answer, I hung up.

13

Virginia

"Hello!"

"Hey Dawn. How ya doing?"

"Okay."

"You don't sound okay. I know I'm calling early. Did I catch you at a bad time?"

"No, no. I just found out that my father-in-law is back in the hospital. He has cancer. I really love him and I hate this for him."

"Sorry. I thought I would call a bit early today. I'm going up to my cabin for a few days. Jake and I need to go fishing. So I will be out of touch. Wish I could take you with me."

"I could use a few days fishing and relaxing." I was smiling, even though Michael couldn't see me.

"Well, who knows, maybe one day you can visit."

"Are you always asking strange women to visit you?"

"Are you strange?"

I chuckled. "Maybe a bit."

"Now that has me curious. Is that strange or kinky?"

"Well, you don't know and I plan on keeping it that way."

"See how you are?"

I could hear some strange noise in the background, something I couldn't make out. Maybe something being moved around. After almost an hour of conversation of this and I finally had to ask. "What's that noise?"

"Oh, I'm just packing up a few supplies for the trip while we talk."

Time always seemed to pass quickly while I was on the phone with Michael. I was at ease now, talking about everything. Well, almost everything. We had not talked about our sex lives. I suppose at our ages that was not something we would do over the phone. Although I wondered what he meant when he asked if I was strange or kinky? Later, I thought that I should have answered him as not strange, not kinky, but I'm not a prude either.

All of a sudden I heard a huge thump on his end. "Holy cow! What was that?"

"Damn it! Hold on!"

I waited for him to come back to the phone. I could hear all sorts of rustling, but couldn't tell just what it was. At one point, I thought I heard a moan and furniture being moved around.

"Sorry about that. A minor problem."

"Oh? Sounded like a fight with a chair," I joked.

"Nope; just me fighting with my backpack."

Not thinking anything else about the strange sounds, I realized it was almost eleven. "I suppose I should let you go. It's late here and I need to get up fairly early and make the trip over to the V.A. hospital. Have fun fishing."

"Take care. I'll call you when I get back."

"Okay, be careful out there in the wilderness. Goodnight."

"Goodnight, pretty lady."

Just as I was pressing the end button, I thought I heard that moaning again, but the line went dead. Maybe Michael was groaning picking up the backpack again.

I put my phone in the charger and headed to bed. I laid there for what seemed hours, forcing the thoughts of John out of my mind. I didn't want to think about him. I really wanted to think about Michael. Too much water under the John Bridge to go back, yet his words of wanting to talk kept seeping into my brain. Damn him after all!

Sleep finally found me and left me with a dreamless night, for which I was grateful. I had enough bad dreams to last a lifetime. I woke rested and ready to make the trip to the hospital. It would be good to see Dad if only it were under different circumstances. Dad had always treated me like a daughter and he wasn't very happy about the circumstances that brought about the divorce from his son.

Sunday morning found the south part of Richmond quiet and with hardly any traffic. That was about the only time of the week you could drive through the city and not find an accident or some kind of traffic jam. Finding a parking spot in the huge hospital parking lot was not as easy as getting there. I ended up parking half way around the building away from the front entrance.

Going to the V.A. hospital always made me sad. So many sick and homeless looking men and women that were defenders of the nation, all in one place. I stopped outside the front doors and lit up a cigarette. A patient in a wheelchair rolled up. "You have one of those to spare?"

"Sure." I smiled as I pulled the pack from my purse. "You know these aren't good for us?"

"Lady, at this stage of my life I really don't give a damn." He took the cigarette, lit it, and blew out the smoke.

"I hear ya." We sat quietly enjoying the sunshine and the cigarettes. I stood to leave, pulled the pack from my purse, and placed it in his lap. "Don't smoke them all at once."

He smiled and laughed. "Geez, they might kill me!"

I walked into the building that had not changed since my last visit. Dad already had two surgeries here and now maybe another. I picked up the phone at the information desk, asked for his room number and the nice voice on the other end announced, "Room 414, cancer wing."

I reached the room, finding it empty. A nurse walking by said, "He's down in X-ray, should be back any minute."

"Thanks," I said as I pulled a chair out from the wall and took a seat. I sat looking out the window, wondering just how bad things were this time. Whatever was going on, I was hoping John would be able to get away from work and travel to visit. I was about to doze off when I heard, "Hey you."

A nurse was pushing him in to the room in a wheelchair and Mom was following. "Hey you back. I thought you were through with this place?"

"Me too." He stood to take the few steps toward the bed. I hated to see just how weak he had become since the last time I saw him only a month ago.

"Who called you?" Mom asked.

I wanted to say that it sure wasn't you, but I held my tongue. "John."

They both looked at me with no trace of surprise. "So, what's going on?"

"They want to take out the other half of the lung." Dad breathed heavily.

"No choice if he wants to live longer." Mom started to tear up.

"Stop crying! It is what it is. After they remove the rest of the lung, I go back on Chemo."

"When will they operate?" I sat back down.

"Probably tomorrow or the next day." Mom sat down on the edge of the bed.

Before I could reply, there was a light knock at the door. We all looked up and saw John standing there. He looked pale and tired.

"Oh, I didn't know you were coming today," I said, trying not to sound hateful, but I really didn't want to see him. For that matter, I wasn't sure if I wanted to see him at all ever again.

"I drove all night. I actually made really good time." He walked over to the bed and hugged them both. "Did I hear right; they are going to operate tomorrow?"

An aide stepped into the room with a lunch tray, sitting it on the bedside table.

"Oh boy, lunch! I wonder if they ran it through the machine down in the kitchen that strains all the taste out of everything." I stood to excuse myself. "I'm going to run down to the cafeteria and get some coffee. I'll be back."

"I could use a cup of coffee, too. Mind if I come with you?" John didn't wait for me to answer; he just headed for the door.

We started walking down the hallway toward the elevator doors. I was doing my best to walk ahead of him, not wanting to look at him. Just as we reached the elevator doors, they opened. I stepped in quickly, John right behind me, and we rode down in silence.

We walked in silence, got the cups of coffee in silence, found a table away from anyone else in silence, and sat. "Are you going to talk to me?" he asked after a few seconds.

"I don't have much to say." I was lying. There was a whole lot I wanted to say, things that still hurt me, things I was having a hard time getting over, and the things that might hurt me forever. This was not the place to unload.

"Coming to see Dad wasn't my only reason for coming here. I wanted to see you. I wanted to talk to you." He wasn't drinking his coffee, just stirring.

"I don't think we have anything else to talk about." I took a big drink of my coffee.

"Well, we sort of do. I really need to tell you something important."

"What can be so important that you couldn't tell me on the phone?"

"We're not divorced."

I looked at him in bewilderment. "What?"

"We're not divorced."

"I heard you. What are you talking about?"

"I never signed the final papers and they were not filed. It's been over ninety days so it's all null and void."

I heard his words clearly, but they were not sinking in like they should. "I never got any mail saying things were void."

"Did you get any papers saying things were final?" John stopped stirring his damn coffee.

"No, but I figured my lawyer had them."

"Nope. We're still married."

"Why would you do that? You are the one that wanted to be not married! You are the one that started dating! You are the one that seemed so happy to be shed of me when I would see you in Birmingham. Sign the damn papers."

"I don't want to. I don't want to be single. I want to move here and start over. I want you!"

People several rows of tables away started looking our way. I supposed we were getting rather loud. I felt the anger taking over my body. "How dare you!"

John reached for my hand. I jerked it back, spilling the two coffee cups. Coffee started running all over the table top. John jumped up, running over to the dish cart and grabbing a towel to sop up the spilled coffee. I stood, grabbed my purse, and headed for the door.

I was out the door as fast as I could move. "Stop!" he shouted.

"John, just sign the papers and leave me alone," I yelled back. I was almost to my car. He must have been looking for my Taurus, because he had parked his Mustang just a few slots down the row from me.

Reaching for the door handle, I felt John come up behind me. "I don't want to leave you alone. I will not sign any papers. I'm moving here in a couple of months. If you want to divorce me, then you will have to do it according to Virginia laws."

"It's always what you want, isn't it, John?" I slid in behind the steering wheel and started the car. "Please tell the folks I will be back in a couple of days. I can't stay here today with you here."

All I wanted to do was go back to the apartment, have a drink of wine, get on the computer or phone, and visit with Michael. Talking to him made me forget about John and the pain that came with any thoughts of him. Only Michael was not going to be available for a few days.

Now I had to figure a way to tell Michael that I wasn't divorced. I was a married woman on the web, looking for something that I didn't know for sure even existed.

Damn it, John!

14

Virginia

"Holy Crap," Cindy said way too loud as she poured a cup of coffee. "You don't look so good. What did you get into?"

"That bad, huh?" Taking another long drink of my almost cold coffee, I looked at her. "I couldn't sleep last night so I came to work early. I have been sitting here drinking coffee and trying to figure out what to do."

Cindy pulled a chair out from the break room table and sat down softly. "What to do? What's going on?"

"Cheese and rice, Cindy." I started to tear up, but held the rush of emotions back. "John showed up yesterday."

"Showed up where?"

"Dad is back in the hospital. The cancer is back and he's facing surgery again. I was visiting him at the V.A. and John walked in. Walked in like he owned the place."

"Crap, what did he have to say?"

"Well the big news, we are not divorced! How about those apples?" I stood to get more coffee.

"What? Are you sure? What did he tell you? What in the……"

"My feelings exactly. WTF! He said he never signed the final papers. In Alabama both parties have to sign the final papers within ninety days or the whole thing is cancelled. I signed my papers before I made the move. With everything that was going on, I guess it slipped my mind that I was never sent the final papers."

"Jesus! Now what?" Cindy reached over and took my hand in a kind gesture.

"He said he was moving here. Said if I wanted a divorce, I would have to file and get one according to Virginia law."

"You do know that he will have to be a resident for at least six months before he can get a divorce here, even if you do the filing, don't you?"

"He said he made a mistake, he wants to start over, that he loves me." Still holding back the tears the best I could, I felt a tear trickle down my cheek. "Damn it."

"What happened to his girlfriend?"

"Don't know, don't care, didn't ask." I was trying my best to convince myself I didn't care. Cindy knew that also, but didn't let on.

We sat there quietly for a few minutes when the front door opened and we heard some of the other women coming in to start the work day.

"Go freshen up. We'll talk more later if you want." Cindy took her coffee from the table, smiled at me, and walked out of the room.

I did as she suggested. I struggled with some makeup, trying to hide the sleepless night that showed through my red eyes and the dark circles under them. It was going to be a long day.

Even though it seemed like I was moving in slow motion, the work day came to an end rather quickly. I had punched my time card and was gathering my things when Cindy walked up. "Sorry I couldn't have lunch with you, but I had to run some errands for Ted. He will be home from D.C. tomorrow."

"That's okay. I wouldn't have been very good company, anyway." I started for the door.

"You want to come over to the house for a bit?"

"I don't think so, but thanks anyway. I'm going to go home, try to figure some things out, and get some sleep."

"Okay, call if you need to talk. I'll be home within the hour."

It's a good thing that the Taurus knew the way home, because driving in rush hour traffic on the south side of Richmond with your mind in other places just wasn't a good idea.

I had just changed out of my work clothes into some shorts and a T-shirt, poured myself a glass of wine, and flopped down in the chair when my cell phone rang. Picking it up, I looked at the caller ID and it was John. I threw the phone across the room and drank down half of the wine.

I picked the phone up on my way back into the kitchen to refill my glass. Making sure I hadn't broken it in the toss across the room, I turned the phone off. Finishing my second glass of wine, I turned the lights off and went to bed. After the sleepless night before, falling asleep with the help of two glasses of wine came easily.

Finding the off button on the obnoxious alarm clock beside my bed wasn't as easy. Now my head hurt. Making my way to the shower, I found myself wondering just how bad things were going to get. Again! The thought of having to file again for a divorce I thought was already final, was making my stomach turn. It wasn't fair that I had to go through this again.

After a few minutes under the hot water, I realized how selfish those thoughts were. Dad was lying in the hospital, having to go through surgery again, and the cancer was back and spreading. That was unfair. I needed to go and see him. "I'll go tomorrow," I said to myself.

"Wow, what a difference a day makes!" Cindy smiled when I walked into the front door at work.

"Yep; I feel much better, thank you." I smiled back.

"I tried to call you last night, but your phone went straight to voice mail."

"Oh, I had turned it off. In fact, it's still off." I reached into my purse, pulling the phone out, and turning it on. The screen lit up with four missed calls. One from Cindy and three from John.

Looking over my shoulder, Cindy whispered, "You going to call him back?"

"No; not today, anyway. Maybe he's gone back to Alabama."

"Maybe he's gone to Hell!" Cindy was laughing.

"Isn't that the same thing?" Now I was laughing. Today would be a better day after all.

15

Montana

Tears streaming down the tall blonde's cheeks, she tried to scream through the duct tape that covered her mouth. Her arms stretched out before her, wrists taped together with a nylon rope connecting her to Michael.

"Make all the noise you want; no one is going to hear you out here." He smiled to himself. He felt the rope go taunt. He stopped and looked behind him, finding the woman flat on the ground. "Get up!" he yelled.

Once she was back on her feet, he could see the fear in her eyes. Beautiful blue eyes that now were red from crying. Her nose was red and running. Snot was dripping down over the duct tape.

"God, you are a mess. It will be good to get rid of you. I won't be much longer." He turned and tugged at the rope. "I need to get rid of you before my new woman arrives from Virginia."

Whistling, he was thinking of how desperate these Internet women were. How easily they were to deceive. A few messages, a few flirts, a few phone calls, and they were all about meeting him. Things were so much easier now to find his prey with Internet dating. No traveling around from city to city to find women. They all willingly came to him. "God, I love this new age of dating," he said with an evil sneer. "No God out here to save your old ass," he sneered as he pulled on the rope.

They walked another half hour when they came upon a clearing in the trees. "Sit down and relax. Don't bother trying to run off. I'm much faster than your old ass."

***

She sat down on the not so hard ground and watched him pull a water bottle and shovel from his backpack. She was so thirsty, but couldn't even ask for a drink with the tape still in place. Still whistling, he started digging into the soft dirt. Finally, after several hours, he took a break and reached for the water bottle, tipping it up and drinking half of the contents down.

"Oh, would you like a sip?"

The only thing she could do was shake her head up and down. He walked over, ripped the tape from her mouth, and put the open bottle up to her mouth. She took the water as quickly as she could, but most of it ran down her chin and down onto her t-shirt.

"Oh, a wet t-shirt contest! You win. Oh, you are the only contestant." Michael was laughing as he placed the tape loosely back over her wet mouth.

Another hour of digging found the sun getting low and a slight chill to the air. "I think we might need a little fire. This digging is taking me a bit longer than I thought."

She sat, watching him gather some sticks and twigs. He stuck a match to the small pile of sticks, which caught fire quickly. He sat next to the fire, now drinking from a flask. *How could this have happened*, she thought? She had checked him

109

out on Google. They had talked, texted, and emailed for almost three months. Everything seemed on the up and up. He was her age. She just turned forty-nine. How stupid had she been? Everything was fine. She had traveled to Great Falls and then to Augusta. They had a very nice time, getting to know more about each other. He had been such a gentleman the two nights before. He had slept on the sofa, not even attempting to make a move, both at his house and at the cabin. All was good until that morning. They had breakfast and he started talking about going on a hike. What a grand adventure that was presented to her while they finished a second cup of coffee. She remembered feeling tired. Then the next thing she remembered was waking up on the sofa, duct tape around her, across her mouth, and a rope around her hands. Michael was on a phone, but he had told her there was no cell phone service up at the cabin. Her phone was off and in her bag, saving the battery for later. Now here she was, watching her own grave being dug. *If only I hadn't got on line, if only I had stayed at home. If only… …*

***

Michael left the fire and flopped down beside her. "I think I have been a gentleman long enough. What do you think?" He took the flask and dripped whiskey onto the front of her t-shirt. The fear in her eyes grew as she shook her head from side to side.

Grabbing the back of her head, he pulled her backward, stretching her out on the ground. Taking a knife from his belt, he cut up the front of her t-shirt, folding the material away from her

110

breasts. "Oh, open front bra, I like those," he breathed as he undid the front clasp. "Not bad for an old gal."

She closed her eyes, praying for this to not go any further, but her prayers would not be answered. He ripped the tape away from her mouth, shushing her at the same time. Before she could say anything, he pressed onto her, kissing her so hard she couldn't get away from him. She felt the skin on her lips break and tasted her own blood.

He finally stopped. "Please, don't do this!" she pleaded.

Laughing, he knelt beside her, jerking her jeans down, then cut her high cut panties from her body. Pinning her still tied hands above her head, she could hear him undoing his belt and zipper. He then forced his legs between her knees. Still laughing, he forced himself into her. She wanted to scream, but she would not give him the satisfaction of feeling her pain. Instead she laid still, tears running down the sides of her head, dripping into her ears. The tears in her ears muffled the sound of his grunting. Thankfully, the excitement he found in the violent act caused him to climax quickly. She felt like her body would never be the same, but it didn't really matter. She knew her time on this earth wasn't long to be had. He stood, fixing his clothes, and threw the now empty flask on to her bare belly. He walked back over to the fire and sat down.

In a painful daze, the blonde woman pulled her jeans up over her bloody, dirt covered body and tried to cover her bare breast. She then curled into a tight ball until he tugged on the rope. "Come on; get up."

She stood, trying to focus through her now swollen eyes. He led her past the still burning fire to the dug up ground. As her eyes came in to focus in the black darkness of the mountains west of Augusta, a Cold .45 was leveled at the back of her head. With a flash from the muzzle, the blonde from the Internet dating site exhaled her last breath, as her body fell into the shallow grave. No one heard the gunshot. No one knew where or when she died.

16

Virginia

That day at the hospital and the next went by just fine. No phone calls from John, which left me thinking he had gone back to Alabama. He was going to leave me alone. I had decided to drive by the hospital after work and visit with Dad. I was on the list for family members to receive updates on his condition so I knew his surgery went well. I had not called in fear that I would wake him up. He needed his rest, which is hard to get when you are in the hospital. Someone is always poking you, getting your vital signs or blood.

Traffic was the usual Richmond bumper to bumper in the rush after work. Some days I wondered why I had ever moved to this place. I hated traffic and the way city people drove. Everyone was always in a hurry and rude trying to get to their destination.

It took me over an hour to make the ten minute drive from work to the hospital. Even though I had not heard from John, I found myself driving around the huge parking lot looking for a Mustang with Alabama plates. I didn't even see a Mustang that looked like his, which put me at ease.

I parked and walked across the large parking lot that stretched out in front of the cancer wing. I was giving it my best to not show how depressed this place made me. Just walking in the door was enough to bring tears to my eyes.

To my surprise, Dad was sitting up in bed when I walked into his room. Mom was asleep in the chair that sat on the other side of the bed. "Hey you," I whispered.

"Hey," Dad labored.

I pulled a chair up to the side of the bed next to the door, trying not to make too much noise so I didn't wake Mom.

"Well, I'm glad to see you are still with us." I smiled.

Dad gave me a good smile back. "You didn't think you would get rid of me that easily, did you?"

We talked about the surgery and discussed how we might talk Mom into going home for a day and get some rest. Without opening her eyes, she smiled. "It's not going to happen. I'm staying right here."

We laughed and since Mom was awake I figured it was a good time to excuse myself. "I really should be going. Is there anything I can get you before I go?"

"I don't think so, unless you have some good wine in your purse." Dad was grinning.

I stood and kissed him on the forehead. "Nope, I'm afraid you are out of luck. I love you. Will see you in a couple of days. Call me if you need anything."

"Goodnight, Honey," he said as he closed his eyes.

Before I could put the chair back by the wall, Mom rose and said, "I'll walk with you."

We walked down the long hallway, passing door after door of ailing veterans, not saying anything. I was about to ask Mom to go down to the cafeteria when she stopped.

"Have you heard anything from John?"

"No."

"I think he went back to Alabama to pack up the house. He told us he's moving here."

"Did he also tell you he never signed the papers?"

"Yes. He said he was moving here to win you back. How do you feel about that?"

I really didn't want to have this conversation with my mother in-law. I figured she would repeat anything I said to John. "I'm not too happy about any of it."

"Oh, but...."

"Mom, I really don't want to talk about this. I'm heading home. Call if you need anything." I kissed her on the cheek and left her standing in the hallway. I didn't look back as I passed through the double doors to the parking lot.

By the time I approached the bridge, traffic was thinned out and there were no traffic jams. I supposed people were now home with their families and dinners were being prepared in the houses I passed by. It gave me a lonely sense of being. I was going home to an empty apartment. I tried to tell myself it was better to be alone by myself than to be alone with someone.

I was just about changed out of my work clothes when my cell phone sounded off. I picked it up, looked at the caller ID. It was John. I did not throw the phone this time. Instead, I laid it gently on the table. As I finished changing into my slouchy after work clothes, I heard the beep telling me I had a voice message. "Cheese and rice, John, why don't you just give it up?" I said aloud.

I dialed the voice mail number, entered my password, and listened. It was John. "Dawn, I wish you would answer my calls. Please call me back when you get this. We really need to talk."

I deleted the message. "Not going to happen," I announced as I placed the phone back down on the table.

It was early and I really didn't want to go to bed. Depression was closing in on me, the walls of the little apartment were moving inward. With only one little light turned on the place seemed dark. Fighting tears, I picked up the phone, tucking it into my pants pocket, turned the light off, and crashed on to the bed. Pulling the quilt up to my chin, I told myself not to cry. I had shed enough tears in my life over men, especially John. As my mother would say, "Enough is enough."

Time slipped away, allowing sleep to overcome me. A muffled ringing woke me. Groggy, half asleep, I wasn't sure from where the noise was coming. I finally reached into my pocket. Without looking I answered, "Hello?"

"Hey! Oh, did I wake you?" The smooth manly voice of Michael came across loud and clear.

"Yes, but that's okay. I fell asleep early."

"I can call you tomorrow; you go back to sleep. I just got home and I wanted to talk to you."

"No, no, that's okay." It really was fine. In fact, it was just what I needed or wanted. I wasn't sure which, probably both. "How was fishing?"

"Jake and I did great. It was so nice up at the cabin. I did a lot of thinking the past couple of days."

"Oh? Pray tell, what about?"

"I think we should make some plans on you coming to Montana for a visit."

"Oh really?"

"Yes, really. I know you don't know me from Adam, but how else are you going to get to know me unless you come and visit?"

"Well, you do have a point."

"Well, at least think about it. Now get some sleep. I'll call you tomorrow. Goodnight."

Before I could answer, he ended the call. I laid the phone on the night stand, pulled the quilt back up, and closed my eyes. Montana seemed so far away, but right now far away was where I wanted to be. In Montana, I wouldn't have to deal with anything but a good time.

17

Montana

We put the supplies from the duffel and backpack into the cupboards and fridge. He had brought a couple more bottles of wine.

"On my hike back up here, I was thinking we should take a day or two and hike farther back into the Lewis and Clark wilderness. We could do a couple days of hard core camping. I think you would really like it."

"More wilderness, huh? This isn't wilderness all around us?"

Laughing, Michael looked at me. "Not really. The deeper we go it's like it was a hundred years ago. And best of all, no people."

"Sure, why not. Will we be able to make a call first so I can let people know where I will be?"

"Why would you want to do that? You're with me. No worries. Besides, no cell phone coverage up here." He was still smiling, but something about the way he asked the question gave me shivers.

"I need to take a shower and then I will rustle us up something to eat. Would you like to join me?"

"In the shower or rustling up some food?" I smiled.

"Both!"

"I think I will pass on the shower. Can I get a rain check?"

"Sure," he said over his shoulder as he turned and walked into the bathroom.

I waited until I heard the water running, then I walked out onto the porch. I sat in the rocker, making myself relax. Something wasn't sitting right with me and I couldn't put my fingers on anything in particular. "Why would you want to do that?" The words kept repeating in my mind. Why wouldn't I? I thought it would be a good idea to let people know where you might be when hiking around unpopulated places. Even back in Alabama when John and I would go camping we always let someone know where we were going to be and when we would be back.

Well, Cindy and Ted knew where I was, sort of. Over the two months that Michael and I had talked and emailed each other, how much information had he really given me about his cabin? He had given me the address of his house in Augusta, but I could have found that on Google Earth. When I had tried to find his cabin on Google Earth, I had no luck just as he had told me I would. From Google Earth I found the roof tops of cabins West of Augusta, but I had no earthly idea which one might have be his.

Ted had a friend that worked in Washington that had connections with military people and their satellites. Even those people couldn't give me any more information. I remembered brushing it all off when we looked at the computer screen, nothing but trees and maybe some old buildings. Green trees and green steel roofs, everything blended together.

That familiar feeling of loneliness was creeping over me as the sun started to sink behind the trees to the northwest. I was sure I didn't want to start off on a hike in that direction. The Bob Marshall was to the West and Northwest. I knew there was hundreds if not thousands of square miles of nothing but square miles in the Bob Marshall. I had seen that on Google and maps. If I wanted to escape this place I would need to head into the opposite direction. "Escape from what?" I asked myself, a little too loud.

"Yes, escape from what?" Michael asked. He was standing in the doorway.

I jumped up out of the chair. "Jesus, you didn't have to sneak up on me!"

"I didn't sneak! I was just watching you rocking in the chair. I thought you were enjoying yourself before you said escape. Are you planning on leaving?"

I felt like I was lying and I suppose I was when I said, "I was thinking on how to escape from danger, like a bear or fire or something."

He reached for me, taking my hand and pulling me toward him. "As long as you don't try and escape me."

He pulled me close to his clean smelling chest, wrapping his arms around me. I looked up into those green eyes which made the escape thoughts melt away. He bent down and kissed me gently. I felt his tongue brush my bottom lip just a bit, just a slight tease. There was no way I could not kiss him back.

After a long slow kiss, I pulled away, smiling. "I don't think we are going to get any food rustled up if you keep kissing me like that."

"Okay, we'll save that for dessert." He gave me that killer smile of his that made his green eyes dance.

We did what I call the kitchen dance. That's when a couple dance around each other in the kitchen, each preparing and cooking something for a meal. I tried not to think of the many times John and I had done that same dance

"We're pretty good at this team work getting dinner done." He grabbed two plates from the shelf. Together we had managed to put together a good looking feast of Quinoa, chicken breasts, green beans, and some garlic bread.

"Yum, that garlic bread smells good. Won't be any vampires here tonight." I was laughing.

"It won't keep me from biting your neck." Michael was laughing, too, while he took a big bite of bread.

I poured some wine and took a stool at the bar next to Michael. It felt like we had done this many times before. I was having a hard time with all the different feelings with this different man. Strange vibes would give away to a comfortable relaxed feeling. Maybe I was over thinking things and should just relax and enjoy what time I had here. How many times would I tell myself that before I could relax?

It was dark by the time we finished dinner and cleaned up the kitchen. Michael poured us some brandy. "Grab a blanket off the back of the chair and let's go sit on the porch. Maybe we'll see some deer or elk."

The mountain evening air was chilly, but the fleece blanket wrapped around my shoulders made me cozy, that and my second sniffer of brandy. We sat quietly watching the tree line when we heard some crackling of some sticks or maybe branches coming from the darkness. I was about to ask if it could be a bear when a huge cow elk emerged from the trees. She started grazing on the green grass that had sprouted up between the rocks. She moved closer to the slightly lit area around the cabin. She stopped munching for a second, lifted her head, and looked into the trees behind her. More crackling of branches. Then a large bull elk, antlers not well developed, poked his head out of the tree line. He took a few steps and joined the cow in the evening meal of fresh green grass.

We watched them eating their way across the open area in front of the cabin. Neither of us moved, not even to take another sip of brandy. I don't think they ever saw us. If they did, they knew we were no threat. They eventually moved into the woods and disappeared into the darkness.

"Wow that was amazing. I have never been that close to an elk." I took a big drink of the brandy as I was now feeling the chill of the night.

"How about I go start a fire? Some nice snuggling and some more brandy sounds like a good idea." Michael stood, smiled, and disappeared into the cabin.

I gave the night a silent good night and joined him. The fire was starting up quickly. Still wrapped in the fleece blanket, I sat on the floor squarely in front of the hearth. The warmth from the growing flames caressed my cheeks. Michael sat down beside me, leaning his back up against the chair behind him. He pulled me over so that I was lying between his legs, my back on his chest.

"Hum, this is nice." I wasn't sure what was heating me up the quickest, the heat from the fire, the warmth of the brandy, or the heat Michael's body was throwing off. It really didn't matter; I was enjoying it all.

Michael started nibbling at my neck. With each little nibbling kiss, I felt goose bumps running down my arms. All of a sudden I realized his excitement pushing on my back. I rose up and turned, kneeling on my knees. "I don't think I'm ready for this. I really need just a bit more time. Please understand."

"I certainly don't want to push you into something you are not ready to deal with. We aren't two teenagers that think there is no time and we are desperate to lose our virginity."

"Well, that boat sailed a long time ago." I was now giggling.

"You and me both. I was fourteen. How about you?"

"Oh, I suppose like most girls my age, I was sixteen, pushing seventeen. Then it was almost another year before I tried again." My mouth felt like someone had poured it full of sand it was so dry. "I need some water."

Before I could stand, Michael was up, heading toward the kitchen. He returned with a tall glass of cold water. I had wrapped the blanket around me and was enjoying the dying fire. I took a long drink of the cold water while Michael placed another log on the fire. "That should do us for a while."

"Does it bother you to talk about your past with me? I mean, it's different in person than on a long distance phone call, don't you think?" Michael returned to his place behind me.

"No, I don't think so. You have been very easy to talk with since the very first time we spoke. I wish I was ready to make love to you again. It has been a long time for me. I guess I'm not as confident as I thought I was when it comes to getting naked at my age."

"From what I have seen, you have nothing to be self-conscious about. Trust me. I don't date young, super model types. I want a woman with some age and knowledge. I want the time right for you. Besides, we have a big day ahead of us tomorrow. A pretty good hike. You will need your energy.

I felt both of our bodies relaxing in front of the fire. I didn't remember falling asleep.

18

Montana

I was not sure what woke me up first, the smell of bacon or Jake licking my cheeks. "Morning Jake." He wagged his tail, gave me another lick, and left. I was still under the fleece blanket on the floor. The fireplace had what was left of a few hot coals from the fire the night before.

"Morning there, Sunshine," Michael called from across the room.

"Hum, morning. That bacon smells really yummy. Do I have time for a shower before breakfast?" I stood, wrapping the blanket around myself and feeling the chilly morning coming in from the opened door.

"Sure. Then after we eat we can get going. I have all our gear packed up and ready."

I made my way to the bathroom, picked out some clean clothes, and jumped into the shower. I let the hot water chase the stiffness from my back away. Sleeping on the floor should probably be left for younger people.

I could hear Michael whistling in the kitchen and talking to Jake. "We'll have a fun day tomorrow, won't we, boy?" Jake's tail was thumping on the breakfast bar. I was wondering what kind of fun Michael had in mind.

I wrapped my head and body in clean towels that had been left out for me. I took out the hair dryer and dried my chopped up hair. I looked in the mirror, still wondering what had gotten into me to do that to my own head. I dressed in some long pants that zipped off just above the knees, which I thought were the best idea for this climate. Hot during the day and just above freezing at night. But then I changed my mind and pulled on a pair of jeans. I tucked a T-shirt into my pants, threw on a light weight fleece shirt, and grabbed some socks and my light weight hiking boots. I grabbed another pair of jeans and some socks.

I opened the bathroom door to find Jake sitting there, waiting on me. "Well, hey Jake. Am I late for breakfast or something?" He wagged his tail, stood, and walked over by the front door and flopped down. "Guess he's ready to get going, huh?"

"Jake is always ready. He loves being outside. He takes off from time to time, but always shows back up. One time he took off from the house in town and was gone for almost two weeks. Came back filthy and hungry. I was worried that something had happened to him. I guess he just gets that call of the wild. Come and eat."

I sat down at the bar where a plate had been set, full of bacon, toast, and eggs. A big cup of coffee sat to the side.

"This looks great," I praised as I started to dig in. I was much hungrier than I had thought. Michael sat down beside me with an identical plate, only it had three eggs instead of two. "Looks like you are hungry, too."

126

"Are you kidding? I can usually eat a horse in the mornings!" he joked between bites. "It didn't take you long to fall asleep. I was playing with your hair, enjoying the view. I looked away for a second, looked back, and you were dead to the world."

"I was not." I was laughing. "Okay, guess I was. Do you have our route planned for our big adventure?"

"No worries, I know this part of Montana like the back of my hand. Don't need any routes or maps."

"No maps? What if we get lost?"

"I won't get lost, don't worry your pretty little head."

"Okay." But I was sort of worried. Just a funny feeling that things just weren't right. I hated it when I got these feelings. In the past they always proved to be something I should have listened to in the first place. This time I just couldn't put my finger on what was making me feel uneasy. I kept brushing it off, thinking I was being silly. It was just that I was with someone new, in different surroundings. I couldn't help but think, *I hope I'm right.*

We finished our food and let Jake lick the plates. I washed the dishes and left them to dry in the drainer. Michael had packed a smaller, lighter weight backpack for me. He helped me into the straps and made sure I was comfortable with the weight. He slung the bigger, heavier pack onto his back, strapped it down, handed me a big walking stick, and looked at Jake and said, "You ready to go, boy?"

Jake bounded off the porch and headed in the direction we had gone before when we went to the falls. Michael whistled for him and started walking almost in the direct opposite direction. Jake came running and I followed along.

I knew there wasn't any phone signal here or probably where we were heading, but I still had put my phone in my pocket. I just felt better with it there. A woman just never knew when she might need to call for help.

"Am I walking too fast for you?" Michael asked as he stopped and turned in the middle of a tiny foot trail.

"No, I'm doing fine." I smiled as I caught up with him. He did have longer legs than me and was covering more ground with each step. "I just have these short legs, remember?"

"I could never forget those legs." He smiled back. He took out a bottle of water and took a small sip. Handing me the bottle, I took a drink, just as Jake came running up to us. Michael gave him a drink, too.

We had only been walking for about an hour, but the landscape had changed drastically. The little foot path we were on was barely visible. The underbrush was much thicker than anything I had seen so far. The trees were taller and the boulders grew in size, too. This really was the wilderness. Our trail could pass as a game trail. One could believe that we were the first non-native people to have walked there.

The beauty of this area was beyond imagination. I had often played with the thought that in a previous life I had been a mountain man, only I didn't believe in reincarnation. I did love the mountains and this might be the only opportunity I would have to be in the midst of the Rocky Mountain Front Range. I was drinking it all in.

We came into a clearing on the top of a high ridge. The view was breathtaking. There was nothing but mountain ridges and trees as far as I could see.

"Doesn't get much better than this, does it?"

"I don't see how it could." This time I pulled the water bottle out of his pack and we shared a drink.

"We have a ways to go before we get to the camping spot I'm thinking about. We should press on," he mentioned as he handed the bottle back to me.

I tucked the water bottle back into my pack and fell in behind Michael. Jake was running wild off to our right. I smiled as I watched him having so much fun just acting like a dog. Almost wild and free. Michael would whistle every now and then to make sure Jake was close.

After making our way along the top of the ridge for what I thought was about a half mile, we started down into a steep draw. I was being very careful so I would not misstep and fall down the side of the ridge. I caught up with Michael and Jake at the bottom where a little mountain stream was flowing still farther down into a gulch.

"We have to make our way up this trail a ways and there is a nice cutout in the side of this ridge, a perfect camping place. Watch your step; it gets tricky here."

"I will," I said, trying to sound confident. I had never been in country this remote and rugged. I was glad I had an experienced hiker leading the way.

After almost a mile of what seemed to be another ten miles of hiking at a steady upgrade, we finally came to a clearing. Michael was right; it was a perfect place to camp. There was a large rock overhang to the left of the clearing. Under the overhang I could see where other campfires had been.

Michael set out packs to the back of the overhang, up against the solid rock wall. I could hear the mountain stream below us where we had crossed and the wind blowing through the pines. A few birds overhead sang cheerfully. Michael started gathering firewood. Jake was helping by picking up smaller sticks and running around the area, dropping them here and there.

After we got a nice fire started, Michael and I set up the small tent he had packed for us to share. It was the size of a small three man mountain tent. After all, we would be sharing it with Jake of course.

To my surprise, there were two logs that had been carved out, making them appear to be lounge chairs. Michael motioned for me to take one and him the other. "All the comforts of home," he quipped as he handed me a cup of hot coffee from a thermos he pulled from his pack.

I took a seat on the carved log, stretching my legs out before me. "This is really nice. You come up here often?"

"Here and a couple of other places, but I think this might be my favorite. The large rock overhang has kept me and my fire dry more than once."

Michael stood and retrieved some items from the large backpack. "Dinner!"

"What do we have? I didn't realize how hungry I am until just now."

I sat and watched as Michael poured some water into a small metal container and sat it on the edge of the fire. Then he poured two freeze dried dinners into a little camping pot. "As soon as the water gets hot enough, we will have dinner. Chicken and noodles!"

It didn't take the water long to boil. He added the freeze dried contents to the pot of water. The smell from the chicken and noodle dish made my mouth water. "Wow that smells really good."

"Ah, you're just hungry from the hike." Smiling, he handed me a small metal camping plate and a fork.

I took a fork full and blew on the steaming noodles. Taking a bite, not really knowing if this was going to taste as good as it smelled, to my surprise it was really good. "Yum, this is good."

We sat in the log chairs, enjoying the fire and the hot dinner. Jake waited patiently for his food, lying between us and the fire. The sun had set behind the rock ridge to our backs and the night was creeping up on us, making the fire and the hot food even better.

While Michael fed Jake, I cleaned up our dinner dishes and made some more coffee. When the coffee was finished brewing, I poured two cups, handing one to Michael. He pulled out a small flask from his jacket pocket, tipping it toward me. "Want a little nip in your coffee?"

"Just a nip! I better keep my senses about me."

"Yes you better." He laughed and he poured a shot into my coffee.

The evening passed slowly, both of us enjoying the campfire and the second cup of Irish coffee. I was feeling relaxed and comfortable. We were touching on every topic from past relationships to the differences of living back East and out West. These were topics we had discussed on the phone long before I had said I would visit Montana. I tried to make mental notes to see if there were any changes in his comments, but I had found none. I was feeling pretty safe in this strangers company. I wondered if he was making the same mental notes regarding my comments.

"It's getting late. The sun doesn't set up this far north until almost ten. I suppose we should get some sleep." Standing, he produced his hand, offering me a pull up. As I came fully erect, he pulled me into his arms. Giving me a strong hug, he whispered into my ear, "You did a good job today, city girl, keeping up with Jake and me."

I pulled back, looking him square in the eye and saying proudly, "I'm not as much of a city girl as you think. Speaking of such, I need to visit the bushes before we get settled into the sleeping bags."

"I'll give you some privacy. I'll go get the sleeping bags ready. Don't go far; stay within the campfire light, just to be safe."

I waited for him to crawl into the tent before I stepped over to the edge of the clearing. I did my business and made my way to the tent where Jake was waiting for me. I crawled into the tent and patted the tent floor as a motion for Jake to join us. He flopped on the end of Michael's bag, and curled up into a small ball. I zipped the flap shut. The fire was still burning enough to give the tent a slight glow on the inside. Michael had unzipped my bag and folded the top down for me. I sat down and took off my boots and tucked them under the foot of the sleeping bag. I stripped down to my T-shirt and panties, folded my jeans, and laid them at the top of the sleeping bag. I would use them for a pillow.

I snuggled down into the bag and zipped up the side. Michael was already zipped in his bag. "Goodnight. I think you will enjoy tomorrow more than today. We will reach real wilderness tomorrow." He leaned over and kissed me softly on the forehead

It seemed only like a minute later both Michael and Jake were snoring. I laid there awake, listening to the fire, watching the flickering glow on the tent walls. There were no other sounds to drown out nature. No reflections of the city lights, no traffic sounds, no laughter of college students walking up and down the city sidewalks during the night. The mountain side was engulfed in total darkness with only stars looking down on the land. Every now and then, I would hear the night sounds of animals in the forest. Nothing sounded large like a bear or elk. I did think I heard the quiet walk of a deer once and maybe some mountain mice skittering around. I finally decided if any kind of danger was to approach, Jake would sound an alarm. Finally, I relaxed my city girl anticipation of possible wildlife attacking.

I was tired that was for sure. But instead of my brain allowing me to sleep in peace, it sent me back to a camping trip years before with John.

I hadn't thought about our trip to northern Georgia for a very long time. Even after all these years, the memory brought a smile to my face. I had forgotten the many survival tactics John had taught me on that trip. At the time, I thought John was silly. Why was I trying to remember them now?

19

Georgia

We had driven up to Chattanooga for a week's vacation. We had picked spring time so the heat and humidity would not suffocate us on our hikes. We had parked our truck on Lookout Mountain and started a three day hike which would take us on trails that soldiers used during the War Between the States. It was an eerie feeling at first, knowing we were hiking on hallow ground. I wondered how many husbands laid down their lives on the path I was walking. The beauty of the land took over and I soon forgot the painful history beneath my feet. Springtime in the Southeast has a beauty all its own.

It was amazing to me that we could walk in what appeared to be deep woods only to come to a small clearing and see roof tops below us. We ran into a few other hikers on the first couple of miles of our hike, but after noon we never saw another person. That was fine with us. We were enjoying the peace and quiet. The hills in Tennessee and Georgia were alive with spring foliage.

We stopped for lunch on a huge rock that overlooked a long valley toward the southwest. The warm spring breeze coming up off the valley floor had the smell of fresh spring flowers. The trees were covered with the little young leaves of spring and there were some Dogwoods flowering. We had already crossed over into Georgia. Most folks think of Chattanooga as only Tennessee, but there is a

Chattanooga, Georgia. Tomorrow we should be along the Alabama state line. We were in no hurry.

Late that afternoon we found a small creek with a nice sandy area to pitch our little two person tent. "You gather some firewood and I'll pitch the tent," John said as he started unpacking his heavier backpack. "Watch for snakes. This warm and this close to water, ya might run up on a Water Moccasin."

"I will." I laid my smaller pack down and started gathering tinder first. In the spring it was easier as winter had left lots of little twigs and pieces of bark all along the creek bank. After I had a good size pile of tinder I started gathering larger limbs that had fallen. Probably from a winter ice storm which happened quite often in this area.

John had always teased me about not having any sense of direction, but I was one hell of a fire builder. He was right. I soon had a good fire going and was ready to start cooking some dinner as he finished with the tent and our sleeping bags. We really did make a good team.

John tried his best that week to teach me more survival skills he had learned in Military school when he was fourteen and during his five years in the Air Force. I would end up screwing something up and then laughing until I cried. Slowly some of the things started to sink into my head. I would have never survived any kind of Military survival training, but I was pleased with some of my new skills.

"Really John? We are in Northern Georgia. How many survival skills does one need here?" I would laugh.

"Holy crap, Dawn! Ya never know when you might need to know this stuff. Now, which way is south?"

I would look around and as always, I pointed in the wrong direction. I thought it was funny. John just frowned and pointed the correct way. I had a feeling he was about to give up on me.

John didn't give up on me. By the time we returned to our truck in Chattanooga, I was able to read a map, find the correct direction, and find things to eat in the woods. He put me to the test again on another camping trip over in the Smokey Mountain National Park. I had led the way that long weekend and never got us lost, not even once. I remembered how proud I was of myself and how John had bragged on me to his friends upon our return.

20

Montana

I woke with a jerk, as Jake started a low growl deep from within. "What's the matter, boy?" Michael asked as he sat up. Jake was trying to stare a hole through the tent door flap. Then we heard the noise, too. "Sounds like a deer running."

"Maybe a bear?" I was afraid to ask. I knew we were in bear country, but I really didn't want to see one up close and personal.

"Not enough noise. You ready to get up?"

"I'm awake now, might as well. I did sleep well once I got to sleep." I didn't want to tell Michael I was thinking about past camping trips with my ex.

"Good. I always sleep well out here. No people around to bother you."

I laughed. "There aren't any people around your cabin either. Don't you sleep well there?"

"Good point." As he finished dressing and sliding his boots on, Michael unzipped the flap and let Jake out. Jake took off like a bullet on the trail after something. "He'll be back in a few minutes. He'll remember breakfast."

"Breakfast sounds good. I'll dress and be right out."

It didn't take me long to dress and poke my head out of the tent door. Michael had already stoked the fire and it was blazing away. He had a small pot of water heating on the edge of the fire. Jake had already returned and was wolfing down some kibble.

I slipped out behind the tent and relieved myself, only to find a hot cup of instant coffee waiting for me when I made my way over to the log chairs. The sun was now shining through the tall trees, warming things up fairly fast.

Michael handed me a small plastic plate full of prepared freeze dried scrambled eggs and some kind of beef. "Lots of protein for our hike today. Hope you like your gourmet breakfast, Montana style."

"Oh, this is very good, no complaints to the chef. In fact, since you cooked, I will clean." I stood as I finished my food.

"Sounds good and while you do that I will pack up things. I need to repack the bags. I will take more of the heavier things. We have some pretty rugged country to cover today. I don't want you being drug down with too much weight." Michael handed me his plate and fork.

"Okay, you know best." I stood and started gathering items. "I'm going to take this stuff down to that little creek we passed and wash this stuff off. Can Jake come with me as a bodyguard?"

"Sure; he's a good one. He'll chase all the critters away. But do talk or sing loudly as you walk down there. Don't want to surprise any bears."

Jake and I made our way to the little mountain creek. Like I was told, I talked very loudly as to alert any bears that a silly human was in their house. Jake was good company, as he never got too far ahead of me. We reached the creek and I found a good size flat rock to balance on, keeping my feet dry while I washed up the few items I had with me. Jake kept running up, splashing me with the water he was kicking up. I finally gave in and threw a stick that he had brought me. "You are one happy dog when someone throws a stick for you, aren't you, boy?"

I threw the stick for him several more times, laughing at him bounding across the small creek. Between throws, I splashed some freezing cold creek water onto my face. "We need to get back. Come on, Jake." I stood there for a moment looking into the creek. "Remember, Dawn, most water runs south. If not South, at least it will always run into other bodies of water. Always follow the water if you get lost. Sooner or later you will find civilization." The words from John years ago were still sticking with me. Why?

Jake brought a different stick back with him. I could see in his big beautiful brown eyes he was hoping I would throw it again. "We have to get back and I have to pee."

I found a large bolder to squat behind while Jake decided he needed to stand right next to me. "Jake, you could at least turn your head and give a gal some privacy." I laughed. Jake didn't move; just stood there wagging his tail, still holding the stick in his mouth.

With all my clothes all squared away, I picked up the few dishes and we started back up the side of the ridge. Jake was running ahead of me as we reached the clearing. "Hey boy! You got yourself a nice looking stick there." Jake had dropped the stick at Michael's feet. Michael picked it up and threw it. Jake took off like a bullet. "I could stand here all day throwing sticks for that dog and I don't think he would ever get tired."

Michael had our packs laid out side by side. He put the dishes into his larger pack. "I didn't give you much to carry; your jacket, pants, sleeping bag, and a water bottle."

"That sure makes your pack heavy. Are you sure?" I picked up my pack to find it much lighter than yesterday. "I think I can carry more."

"That's okay. We have some rugged land to cover today. I would feel safer if I carried the heavier load." He helped me get my pack on and secure. He, on the other hand, needed no help. In what I would consider a sideways backward stoop, one arm through the strap and the backpack swung into place, one easy move.

"I need to learn how to do that! I might need to do that on my own one day." I smiled.

"Practice, just practice." He smiled as he looked around for Jake, who was standing on the other side of the clearing. "There he is. He knows the way."

We left the clearing and started an upgrade hike. The trees were getting fewer and fewer between while the ground under us turned to solid rock. Within minutes, we were above the tree line and I could feel the altitude reminding me that I lived at almost sea level in Richmond. I could feel my lungs wanting more oxygen. I stopped to catch my breath.

"You okay?" Michael stopped, too, and Jake came running back to where I was standing.

"Yes, just need to catch some air. This flat lander isn't used to this altitude." While I was stopped, I took out the water bottle and took a sip. "You want a drink?"

"Nope, I'm good." Michael turned and pointed to a mountain top. "See that ridge over there? That's where we are going. It's a hard hike, but it's worth every step."

"Looks like a lot of up and down hiking from here."

"It is, but we'll make it, probably tomorrow. Then we'll make the loop. That way back is an easier hike." He waited for me to catch my breath before we started up again.

The morning passed rather quickly, for me anyway. We hiked up and down the ridges, in and out of the tree line. When we would be out of the trees, it seemed like I could see to Washington State, if I knew which direction I was looking. I was placing all my trust in Michael since I had not seen what I thought looked like a trail since we left the first clearing. We had kept to the high points, not crossing any creeks. Not even a little run off trickle of a creek. I figured it was too late in the summer for any kind of melting snow to be running off.

The land was indeed getting more rugged. We were walking in more rock than anything else. I was happy when Michael stopped at a large boulder that had a flat top and an easy climb up. Standing on the top of the boulder, Michael shouted, "Come on up here. This is a great place for a rest and some lunch." I reached the bottom of the boulder and accepted his hand and the help up. The flat top of the boulder was warm from the sun. I sat down and stretched my legs out straight in front of me. The heat from the rock felt good on my back of my legs. I was happy I was in fairly good shape. Walking and riding my bicycle all over Richmond had paid off, although the up and down hiking was taking its toll on my legs. They were so tired. I needed to rest them for a bit.

"How about some peanut butter crackers for lunch?"

"Oh, that sounds good. Hiking around up here makes ya hungry for sure." I smiled as he handed me two packs of the yellow crackers. Michael had two packs also. We both shared the second pack with Jake. We all had long drinks of water and then relaxed, stretching out on the rock.

I put my backpack behind my head for a pillow, and my cap was lying over my eyes as I was drinking in the warm sun. I could have melted into the rock for a good long nap. I was about to doze off when Jake started licking my cheek. I tried to push him away, but he didn't give up. "Stop it, Jake!"

"Oh, come on. Jake says it's time to get going." Michael was standing at my feet with his pack already on his back and secured. As I stood, Michael reached out and ran his fingers through my hacked up hair. "Too bad I did that to your hair."

"What?" I wasn't sure, but it sounded like he said he had cut my hair. "What did you just say?"

"I said it was too bad you did that to your hair. What did you think I said?" Michael sounded, startled to my question. But he didn't look startled.

"Never mind; I misheard you." I put my cap back on my head and picked up my pack. This time I swung it over one shoulder and up into place with my left arm hitting the left strap just right. I secured the waist belt. "Hey! I did it by myself! I'm ready."

21

Virginia

"Ted, someone's at the front door. Would you go see who it is?" Cindy yelled from the bathroom. Ted didn't answer her, but she heard his feet heavy on the stairs. She heard the front door open, then mumbling.

Ted yelled up the stairs, "Cindy, come down when you're finished getting dressed! We have company!"

"Company, great! It's my freaking day off; I don't want any company! Who in the hell could be here this time of the morning? I just wanted a hot shower to start my day," she grumbled all the way from the bathroom door, into the walk in closet, and then across the bedroom to the dresser.

Cindy dressed in a T-shirt and jeans. Sliding her feet into some old mules, she made her way back into the bathroom to do something with her hair. "It's my day off; you get a pony tail today," she grumbled some more. "Good enough. Maybe whoever is downstairs will be scared off after getting a look at me!" Now she was laughing.

Making her way down the stairs, she could hear two men talking in the kitchen. Maybe it was a friend of Ted's, she thought. Cindy rounded the corner and to her surprise, she saw the visitor was none other than her best friend's ex-husband. "John!"

"Hey Cindy. Sorry to barge in on you on the weekend. You and Ted are the only people I know to see about some things."

"Ted, I need coffee. John, I don't know what you are talking about. We only met you once and we really don't know you. We are Dawn's friends."

Ted handed Cindy a large cup of coffee. "Why don't we all have a seat? John needs to tell you a few things. It sounds serious."

"What sounds serious?" Cindy was suspicious.

"Have a seat John," Ted said as he pulled out three chairs from the kitchen table. The three of them took seats, Ted and Cindy sitting beside each other and facing John.

"I'm not sure where to start," John exhaled noisily.

"How about the beginning?" Cindy wasn't really in the mood for this, but now she was curious.

"You surely know by now that I have not signed any divorce papers and, in fact, Dawn and I are still legally married, right?" John looked straight into their questioning faces.

"Yes, we know that and Dawn's not real happy about that, but that's really none of our business." Cindy was getting impatient. Ted patted her hand in a manly signal for her to allow John to speak.

"I guess that's true. I begged Dawn to give me a second chance. I was willing to quit my job and take an early retirement so we had start over money. She wasn't too happy with the thought."

"Do you blame her?" Cindy asked while Ted patted her hand a little harder. This time Cindy pulled her hand away and tucked it into her lap.

"After several phone conversations, I decided that I was going to make the move no matter what. At least that would give me some more time to work on her about us trying again. If I moved here she would have to file for divorce in Virginia. We both would have to be residents for a year, not six months as we thought. So I moved. I've been here several weeks. Dawn didn't know." John took a drink of coffee, almost waiting for Cindy to say something. But this time she was quiet.

"She said that she had found someone else, or at least it was a male friend. She didn't know where the situation was going. I can't say that I blame her. I have been a jerk to say the least. All I want to do is make things up to her and be the man she deserves. I just need time to prove it to her." John took a long drink of his coffee.

"I don't know that you can win her back," Cindy said with a sad tone.

"I know that, but that's not what has me so concerned. I'm worried about her and this vacation to Montana."

"What do you mean by that?" Ted suddenly asked.

"It took some doing, but our last conversation before I moved she told me she was going on vacation. She finally told me the name of the man she was going to meet. She wouldn't give me many details. The only thing she said was that he was on-line, his name was Michael Conrad, and he was a gunsmith. I have been doing a lot of research. I just wanted to go over what I found out and see if Dawn told you the same things about this Michael guy."

"I was the one that found Michael on-line, on MrPerfect.com. It started as a joke, something to get her mind off of you. She was pretty miserable. She needed something to distract her," Cindy said, looking John straight in the eye.

"Well, she was distracted alright and I can't blame her. I can give you all sorts of excuses why I lost my mind, but what good would that do? I was deep into a case when I learned she actually moved to Virginia. My folks told me. So many nights I tried to find the courage to call her, but I always chickened out. Then I started drinking my sorrows away. But none of that matters now. What matters is this Michael guy. "

"She has been talking to him for several months. She researched his website and his Facebook site. Lots of emails, too. So what seems to be the problem other than your ego and losing her?" Cindy was about to lose her tempter.

"Do you know where she is right now?" John asked.

Cindy and Ted said, "Montana," simultaneously.

"What would you think if I told you Michael Conrad the gunsmith died several years ago in a car crash in Idaho?" John slid some printed papers across the table toward them.

"I would think it was a different Michael Conrad." Cindy stood to get another cup of coffee.

"I thought so, too, at first, but the more I looked into it, the more there was to look into. Do you know where in Montana she is staying?"

"She flew into Great Falls. Michael was to pick her up and they were driving to his place in a town west of there. I have it written down, but I think it was Augusta. The note is upstairs on my desk." Cindy turned and headed down the hallway.

"John, this all sounds sort of cloak and dagger." Ted said as she made her way to their bedroom, but she could tell he was trying not to let his concern show.

Cindy found her little day planner in her purse and started thumbing through the pages. She could feel the panic creeping up into her throat. "Screw this!" She picked up her cell phone, tapped the photo of Dawn, and pressed call. Shortly the phone was dialing. One ring and the phone went straight to Dawn's voice mail. "Hey, you know who you called. Leave a message and I'll get back to you shortly." Then the beep.

"Dawn! It's Cindy. Please call me as soon as you get this. It's important! Love ya."

"Well, that doesn't make me feel any better. Maybe she's just out of signal range. After all, it is the wilds of Montana. She'll be home in a couple of days," she mumbled to herself.

Cindy returned to the kitchen, grabbed her coffee, took a drink, and started thumbing through the day planner. "I tried to call Dawn while I was upstairs, but it went straight to voice mail."

"From what I know, that shouldn't be much of a surprise. Sounded like they had lots of fishing and camping planned." Ted was doing his best to instill some confidence in his statement.

"Here's the information. She flew into Great Falls and they were going to Augusta, MT where Michael lives. But she didn't give an address. How big can Augusta be?" Cindy thought Dawn had given her Michael's cell phone number, but she couldn't find any numbers in her notes.

"Let's see; I'll Google it," Ted said as he typed into his phone.

John beat him to the draw. "It says here that, Augusta, Montana has three hundred and nine people. They don't even have a police department. County Sheriff polices the area. County seat is Helena." John shut his phone off.

"Okay, let's think this out a bit, before we go into panic mode." Cindy walked over to a kitchen cabinet drawer and pulled out a note pad and pen.

John started talking while Cindy jotted notes. "When she told me she was talking and emailing a man in Montana, of course, I was jealous. Remember I was begging for her to give me another chance. When she told me his name, I started doing a little investigating. You have to remember after twenty some years of being a cop, I'm pretty good at this kind of stuff. I found his

150

website and his Facebook site. All looks on the up and up, unless you start digging deeper."

"Should I be getting scared?" Cindy asked softly.

"I am," John continued. "I thought it was sort of funny with our history that she would be interested in a gunsmith. Okay, not really funny, but interesting. His website is very professionally done. I think it really is on the up and up. Doing a little more digging, I learned that Michael Conrad didn't live in Montana, but was a resident of Idaho. So, I started looking into records."

"Wait a minute. Maybe his website just wasn't updated when he moved to Montana?" Ted asked.

"That could very well be, but I started making some phone calls. It seems that Michael Conrad was killed in a very strange car accident over three years ago."

"Three years? Who told you that?" Cindy was feeling sick to her stomach. *Too much coffee*, she thought.

"I called the Idaho Falls Police Department. According to what I found out, the accident happened between Idaho Falls and Swan Valley. Story goes that Michael had been down in Jackson Hole Wyoming for a gun show over a long weekend. On Sunday night he was driving back home and missed a turn, ran down an embankment into a shallow creek. Broke his neck. Dead at the scene. There are a lot of questions about the accident that have never been answered. He had his seat-belt on and the embankment wasn't very big.

151

The coroner ruled it as an accident. However, he also said there was no way the accident should have broken his neck. Michael was a large, well-built man, exercised every day, hiked and was very active. But there were no signs of foul play. I asked the detective to send me the accident photos and the coroner's report. From everything I saw, I would have to agree, the accident shouldn't have killed anyone. But on the other hand, stranger things have happened. Sometimes it's just the way things happen, no rhyme or reason."

"So if Michael Conrad is dead, who is Michael Conrad in Montana?" Cindy asked with tears building up in her eyes.

"Honey, don't get upset yet. There has to be a good explanation." Ted reached for Cindy's hand.

"I can't help it. I was the one that encouraged her to look at Mister Perfect!"

"Look, you didn't force Dawn into doing anything. If it is anyone's fault, I'll take the hit on this. If I hadn't been acting like a total bonehead, we wouldn't have separated in the first place. If I had kept on being her Mr. Perfect, she wouldn't have gone looking someplace else!" John was hanging his head, ashamed.

"What can we do?" Cindy asked.

"I'm going to try and find out who this Michael Conrad person really is and where he lives. I'm going to really start digging. When will Dawn be back?"

"She's due back this coming Saturday. I'm supposed to pick her up at the airport. But maybe she will call when she gets the messages. She has to come back to civilization to get on the plane!"

John stood. "Okay, I'm going to keep looking into this. If you hear from her, please let me know. In the meantime, we wait."

Cindy and Ted walked John to the door, all shaking hands with a promise to stay in touch. No one wanted to acknowledge their fears. John smiled, turned, and walked toward his car. Ted shut the door, only to turn and see Cindy breaking down.

"Don't cry, Honey. For all we know, this is just a bunch of coincidences. There can be two Michael Conrads. Dawn will be fine. We'll hear from her soon. Stop blaming yourself."

But the tears only came stronger.

22

Montana

I followed along behind Michael a good ways. I was having trouble concentrating on where I was walking. I was sure I hadn't heard him incorrectly. His words kept ringing into my ears. He did say he was sorry he cut my hair! Why on earth would anyone do that to someone? Was it a sick joke and afterward he didn't have the nerve to tell me what he had done?

Then for some odd reason a conversation between Joan, Patty, and I came to mind. We had been out at our usual curing the hang-over breakfast when someone mentioned a killer in Detroit.

"Did you see the news last night?" Joan had asked.

"Nope, I was trying to clean up before we went out. It was on, but I wasn't paying attention." I poured another cup of coffee for everyone.

"They caught the guy that was killing those working girls down on Telegraph Road. What a sick bastard." Joan took a deep breath. "He was picking up the girls and taking them to his place to kill them. But first he would put their hair up in ponytails, cut them off, and then shave their heads before he killed them. That's why all the girls were bald."

Patty was speechless, but I asked, "What was that all about? Did they say?"

154

Shaking her head, Joan explained, "The cop they interviewed said he was keeping the ponytails for trophies. They found over twelve pony tails all arranged on a board. Like I said, sick bastard."

"Hey! Why did you stop?" Michael yelled down at me. He was ahead of me a good twenty yards and up higher on a rocky ridge.

I had stopped hiking and was just staring at the ground. Fear consumed me. What if Michael had cut off my pony tail for a trophy and then for fun chopped up what was left? I couldn't take another step. Jake came running down the slope, his tail wagging with a look on his fur face as if he was wondering why I had stopped.

"Dawn! What's wrong?" Michael screamed at me.

"Ah, nothing! I...I... just thought I saw something. I'm coming!" *How lame that sounded*, I thought.

Michael waited for me to catch up with him near the top of the rocky ridge. I was watching my footing as there were a lot of loose fist size rocks. As I walked, smaller rocks rolled down the ever increasing slope.

"You shouldn't get that far behind. Yell at me when you want to stop. Maybe I should tie a rope around you so I can keep you with me?" He laughed, but the thought being tied to him didn't appeal to me at all. Dear God, what if my hair was in a ponytail on a trophy board. I could feel my pulse racing and I didn't think it was from the incline of the hike. It was from the fear building

155

within me. I needed to get a grip on my fear and stop thinking bad thoughts.

It took almost two hours for us to make it over to the next ridge. I had been trailing behind a good distance, but I finally caught up to Michael in a little clearing. We both had been pretty quiet, with me only answering his polite questions. "You need to rest? You want some water? Are you doing okay?" Finally in the clearing, he stopped and dropped his pack. "I think we should camp here tonight. Nice clearing, plenty of firewood. Look good to you?"

"Sure. I will gather the firewood and start a fire," I said as I dropped my pack. I got my water bottle out and took a good drink.

"Go easy on the water. We have a half days hike tomorrow to get to water. After that, we will have more water sources than we need."

I sat the water bottle down next to my pack and started picking up tinder and small branches. Just like before, Michael set up the tent and spread out the sleeping bags. All seemed well. Maybe I was letting my imagination get the best of me.

I returned with kindling and an arm full of branches to start the fire. I arranged some rocks to form a small fire pit, placed the branches inside the little pit area, and started the tinder. As the flames grew, I gathered larger branches for the evening's fire. When I returned with them, Michael was already heating water for our dinner of freeze dried chicken and noodles. He had also moved two good size rocks near the fire so we didn't have to sit on the ground.

"You have been awfully quiet today. Is there something wrong?" Michael handed me one of the pouches of hot noodles.

"No; just trying to pay attention to where I was walking. I don't feel as sure footed in all this loose stuff as you do. Makes me nervous when I'm walking while little rocks fall down the slope a hundred and fifty feet below. It doesn't seem to bother you, though. You hike like you are part Mountain Goat." I tasted the chicken and noodles, finding the dish delicious. "Yum, this stuff is good."

"Yes it is, compared to the freeze dried stuff we had fifteen years ago. You are right to step carefully. I will try not to hurry you tomorrow. I forget that I do this kind of hiking all the time and my guests do not."

"Ah! Guests you say? So you do bring other women up here to dazzle them with the wilderness?" I was hoping that question didn't sound as probing as it was.

"Well, I think I told you I have had a woman or two up here. Maybe three or four." He was smiling.

"Maybe five or six?" I tried to laugh.

"Oh, are you jealous?" He laughed.

"Maybe a bit. Who wouldn't be jealous of anyone spending time up here? This is the most beautiful country I have ever had the pleasure to hike. Don't get me wrong, Tennessee and Georgia have some wonderful hiking areas. Well, for that matter, the whole Southeast. But this is so different, so wild, and even deadly." I finished my noodles and threw the pouch into the fire.

"Yes, it can be deadly. One could dump a body here and the authorities wouldn't find it for years, maybe never." Smiling, he stood and threw his empty pouch into the fire. Then he put another large dead branch on the flames. "How about some deadly tea?"

"Deadly?" I swallowed.

"Okay, killer tea! I brought a special blend and a little brandy to spice it up."

"That sounds wonderful. I'll feed Jake while you make the tea." I retrieved Jake's folding bowl and his kibbles from Michael's pack. Jake watched me, his tail wagging wildly. "You hungry, boy?"

We sat watching the fire and drinking our spiked tea. The brandy was calming my frayed nerves. "You know tomorrow we need to start thinking about heading back. Saturday is coming up faster than I thought. Do we need to spend the night in Great Falls for me to catch the early flight?"

"I hadn't given that much thought. I guess Saturday is looming. What will happen if you don't make it back on Saturday?" Michael asked, staring into the fire.

"What do you mean? Not make it back? I have no choice; I have a job. I need to be back to work on Monday!" I swallowed the last of my tea.

"Well, what if you didn't go back? Would someone be looking for you right away?"

"Well, of course I have people that would look for me. My friends and my job. Why would you even ask such a thing?" I felt myself feeling warm either from the brandy or from fear. I didn't want to sound scared. I tried to joke. "Have you decided to keep me here?"

"Well, you never know what might happen out here. Lots of people from back East come out here and they are never seen again. We wouldn't want that happening to someone that would have the Feds poking around out here, looking for bodies." He was laughing.

I jumped up so quickly, I startled Jake. He jumped up, looking around as if something was about to happen. I dropped my cup as I stepped back from the fire. "Jesus, Michael! Are you trying to scare the crap out of me? Well, if you are, you're doing a damn good job! What the hell?"

"Hey, I was just saying, that stuff happens," Michael blurted out.

I cut him off quickly, "If you are going to talk crazy crap like that, trying to scare me, then you can just shut up. That's not funny. I'm going to bed!" I turned and stomped off toward the tent, Jake following me.

I unzipped the door and crawled into the tent. Jake made his way inside with me and flopped down in the middle of Michael's sleeping bag. I removed my boots and crawled into my bag. I didn't bother undressing. I was too mad and too scared to think of anything except the question of what if I didn't return. Michael didn't know it, but I doubted if anyone would come looking for me

159

anytime soon. Maybe not ever. I was fighting tears of fear when I heard Michael coming through the tent door.

"Hey, I didn't mean to upset you. I was just making conversation. Tomorrow we will start making our way over to the trail that cuts back toward the cabin. We can go into Great Falls on Friday so you can make your flight on time."

I had my back to him. I didn't bother to turn to face him; I just mumbled, "Fine," like I was already half asleep. However, sleep wouldn't come for what seemed like hours. I laid there trying to figure a way to protect myself in case Michael was not who I thought he was. If he was some kind of monster. I rubbed my whacked up hair as I fought the tears. Jake and Michael were asleep when I lost the fight. I felt the tears well up into my eyes and slowly make their escape. I don't remember when I finally lost the fight to stay awake. I believe it was only the brandy that allowed me to sleep at all.

I woke to silence. I raised my head so see Michael and Jake still sound asleep. The light inside the tent seemed to be glowing. I unzipped my sleeping bag, crawled over to the door, and unzipped it, folding it open. No one moved, although Jake was watching me. I grabbed my boots and stepped out of the tent. The campfire was still glowing and the mountain sky was glowing a soft purple as the sun was just coming up. I slid my feet into my boots and made my way over to the fire. There were a couple of limbs that we hadn't used the night before. I grabbed both of them and set them on the hot left over coals. Taking a small stick I stirred the embers and the limbs caught to flames in a matter of seconds. I smiled to myself. John often called me the fire starter from hell. It was a given talent.

I poured a little water into the little camping pot and placed it on the edge of the fire. Coffee would taste really good this cool mountain morning. I was glad I had long pants on. I reached for my pack and pulled out a hoodie. The extra material felt nice in the cool air. I took a little walk to the other side of a big boulder off to the left of the tent to relieve myself. After as I rounded the boulder, I saw Jake making his way toward the fire and Michael was standing outside the tent door, stretching.

"The water should be hot in a few minutes for some coffee." I smiled.

"Jake and I were wondering where you got off to. I saw you had the fire going. I figured you didn't run off on me," he slid into his boots, tucked his shirt into his jeans, and headed to the fire.

As I reached the edge of the makeshift fire pit, I asked, "Where would I run off to? I have no idea where in the world we are." I turned and pointed to the sun that was now peeking over the trees. "Well, I do know that's East. But that doesn't help me much."

"No need to run. I would find you, anyway." He laughed.

Not wanting to get into a conversation like the scary one we had the night before, I changed the subject. "Is the water hot enough for some coffee?"

Michael handed me two cups and the instant coffee pouch. I shook what looked to be a couple of teaspoons of dried coffee into each cup. Michael then poured hot water into each. I looked over the edge of my cup as I took a sip. Michael was looking over the top of his cup also. His eyes were smiling at me.

"Do you want something to eat or just some coffee?"

"Just coffee for now."

"Good, we can get going here shortly. We have another big day ahead of us since you are in a hurry to get back to civilization."

"No hurry, just responsible. Can't we go back the way we came?"

"Would take too long. We are way over half way through our hike. It's just that this is the hardest part, and then the hike gets easier. Going to see what you're made of today."

We finished our coffee, packed up our gear, and started hiking toward what I thought was the North.

23

Montana

We came to a large clearing at the top of another ridge covered with white rocks of all sizes. The walking was slow for me and it took me a minute or two to catch up with Michael and Jake. I thought I got a glimpse of a trail below us, but I wasn't sure if it was a game trail or human trail. As I approached my two hiking companions, Michael noticed I was looking down at the lower clearing.

Grabbing my upper arm, he pulled me close to him and snarled, "What are you looking at?'

I tried to pull away, but he only tightened his grip. "Hey! Not so hard!"

For a moment there was a hardened glaze in his eyes that caused fear to run through me. He released my arm and apologized, "I'm sorry. I didn't mean to grab you so hard. I don't want you sliding down there." He tilted his head in the direction of the steep slope.

"I'm fine! Don't grab me like that. I don't like being grabbed!" I tried to sound tough, but the fear was leaking out of my throat. Michael laughed and started walking. The trail below us disappeared into the undergrowth. I was so lost.

We walked for hours in the same direction, staying on the very top of the long ridge. The hiking seemed to get harder with every step. More loose rocks falling down the steep inclines. I would watch them until they fell from sight. There were times when we would stop for a drink that I was sure I could hear the faint sound of a small mountain creek. "Water runs toward civilization," kept ringing in my head.

"When will we run into the trail that takes us back to the cabin?" I asked in hopes we would be there shortly.

"Well, we're not going to make it today. We haven't made good enough time. If we are lucky, we will get there tomorrow." Michael was smiling, but it looked more like a sneer. My imagination was getting the best of me.

"Tomorrow? We need to be getting back to the cabin and back to Augusta tomorrow. Am I going to be late?"

"Yep. Very late. But it's still early enough we can make it a little further before we need to camp for the night." Michael turned to start walking then stopped. He turned back toward me, smiling. "I think you can suffer through another night with me."

"I wouldn't call is suffering. It's been very lovely up here, but it's time I get back. I have people waiting on me back home."

"They'll get over it."

I wanted to scream, but there was no one within hearing distance that I could tell. My best bet was to keep walking and keep my mouth shut. All of Michael's comments were only fueling the fire of fear growing within me.

We hiked for what I thought was a half mile when we veered off to the right, moving downward from the top of the ridge. The walking was a bit easier as there were fewer loose rocks to slide out from under us. We came to a small flat place on the side of the mountain.

"This will do. Let's make camp here." Michael threw his pack down and started unpacking just like the nights before. I took that as my cue to gather fire wood. I set my pack down, pulled out my water bottle, and took a long drink.

"I'll gather some firewood."

"Watch your step. Anything off this flat spot is pretty much a long way to the bottom. The late afternoon shadows will trick your eyes. Don't want you to fall to your death." He never looked at me, but I felt like that was a joke.

"Well, I don't want to fall to my death either. I'll be very careful." I started picking up what little twigs and sticks I could find in the mostly rocky area. I ventured to the outer edge to see the land falling away in an almost vertical drop. I was feeling trapped. There was no possible way I could escape once the sun went down, and how would I escape in the light of day? I had no idea where I was and Michael seemed to know the area like the back of his hand. I resolved that the only thing I could do was to play nice.

I gathered a large armful of fallen limbs and headed back to the center of the clearing. Michael had already erected the tent and placed our sleeping bags inside. The dinner supplies were waiting for fire. I tried to be cheerful as I began making a fire pit with small rocks. It wasn't long before I had a nice fire burning.

"You are a great fire starter. You would do well on your own in the wilderness," Michael said as he prepared our freeze dried dinners of more chicken and noodles.

"Well, that would be good if I had any sense of direction. That's one reason I don't do hikes alone." I smiled, but it wasn't genuine. Smiling was my way of playing nice, hoping he couldn't see through my attempt.

We finished our dinners as the sun set and the night cooled quickly. The only light was the glow from the fire. "Excuse me; I need to relieve myself." I stood to go find a private place.

"Don't go far. As you saw while gathering wood, it's a long drop if you step the wrong way."

"Yes, I saw that. I'll just go behind the tent."

When I returned, Jake and Michael were already inside the tent. I hoped that he was as tired as I was and there would be little or no conversation. The more he talked, the more fear crept into me. I needed a clear head.

I opened the tent flap and backed into the tent, sitting on the edge of the sleeping bags with my feet outside. I took my boots off and placed them over by the side wall, within reach in case I needed them in a hurry. I zipped the door flap and scooted my butt up toward the top of the sleeping bag. The bag was totally unzipped. I know I had zipped it up this morning before we packed things up. I pushed the top downward in order to slip my feet into the bag. I was feeling around for the end of the zipper when Michael sat up.

"Having problems?"

"No, just can't find the end of the zipper." I was still fumbling around at the bottom of the bag.

"Here, let me help," he almost whispered. He reached across the middle of my bag, but instead of finding the zipper, he tore the bag off my legs. "You still have all your clothes on. Why is that?"

I tried to recover the sleeping bag that had been ripped from my hands. "I felt cold tonight."

In one sweeping motion, I was pushed backward, flat on my back. Michael was on top of me, pressing himself against me. "Let me see if I can warm you up."

I tried to say no, but his mouth was on mine before I could utter a word. I tried to turn my head, but he grabbed both sides of my head, keeping me from moving. He kissed me hard, forcing his tongue deep into my mouth. I tried to bite him to only have him put pressure on the sides of my skull. "Don't even try that, bitch!"

He placed his forearm across my neck to hold me in place. I was trying to struggle out from under him to only have him press harder. I was afraid he would cut off all of my air. He unzipped my jeans and started tugging at them, pulling them down one side at a time. Soon they were down past my knees, along with my underwear. He then sat on my thighs, one leg on each side of me. In the glow of the campfire, I could see his teeth. I couldn't tell if he was smiling or sneering at me. He pulled my sweatshirt off over my head and tore open my shirt. I was trying to stop him, but against his long arms and strength, I was fighting a hopeless battle. He struck me with the back of his hand. I could feel blood running from my mouth and down my chin. I saw a few stars as I tried to blink my eyes back into focus.

"Michael, stop. Please stop! We don't need to do this, like this. I thought we weren't going to rush things?" I could hear myself whimpering.

"I'm done waiting on you! You are just like all the other bitches!" With that, he ripped my bra from my body. I shut my eyes tight. I started kicking my legs, only to make Michael laugh.

I heard him unbuckle his belt and unzip his jeans. He grabbed both my hands and pinned them above my head. I was no match for his strength. With his body weight, he spread my legs so that he was now between my thighs. He let go of my hands so he could push my jeans down further and took them off my left foot. Now he had me right where he wanted. He grabbed the back of my hip, pulling me upward him and then thrust himself into me. I couldn't help but cry out. White hot pain ripped up through the middle of my body. I was scratching his chest, trying to cause him pain with no success. John had always told me to go for the eyes if I was ever attacked. But my arms were not long enough. My fighting only seemed to excite him more. This wasn't supposed to be happening. I tried to relax. If I could relax and not fight, there would be less tearing, less pain. I lay there, pinned to the bottom of the sleeping bag, trying not to cry, trying not to fight. I thought he would lose interest. When I stopped fighting and scratching, he bent down and bit my shoulder, making me try to escape. I couldn't help but cry out again.

His excitement grew into a frenzy, which was good for me as within just a couple of minutes he was done. He exploded into a crazed orgasm of rage. I still lay as still as possible. I could feel blood and semen on my thighs. As he finished, he back handed me again on the side of my jaw. A few stars, then blackness.

I felt cold as I started to come around. I could still taste blood in my mouth. I wanted this all to be a bad dream, like waking up in a strange place with my hair all hacked off. Only that wasn't a dream and neither was this. I slowly opened one eye. The tent was dark with just a slight glow from the dying campfire. I tried to open my left eye, only to find it almost completely swollen shut. I managed to raise my head enough to look around. I was alone in the tent. My hand ran along my naked, bruised body. I tried to sit up to find my clothes. My jeans and underwear were still on my right ankle. I managed to get my left leg into the legs of both my underwear and jeans, pulling them up. It hurt to move, but I raised my hips up so that I could pull my jeans into place. I felt around for my shirt and sweatshirt. They were by the edge of the tent wall near my head, along with my bra. I wanted to clean myself, but knew better. I ran my hands down my belly to feel thick stickiness on my skin. I knew what I was feeling, but decided not to think of how it got there while I was unconscious, as that thought was making me feel like I wanted to vomit. I managed to get everything back on. Just the weight of my clothing caused the bite on my shoulder to send pain down my arm. All I could smell in the tent and on my body was the musk of his rape. With all that I could muster, I got to my hands and knees to look out the tent door. As I did, I could feel the wetness of him between my legs. "Don't get sick," I told myself.

Michael and Jake were sitting out near the fire. Jake was asleep, but Michael was playing with a stick, poking and stirring the hot embers. He placed a few limbs on the coals, catching them on fire. He then stretched out beside the growing fire, hands behind his head, looking relaxed and satisfied. My stomach turned again.

Very slowly, I lay down and pulled the sleeping bag over me. I was shaking. Shaking from the cold and the pain. Tears started filling my eyes. "How stupid I have been," I said to myself. I had to rest and get my strength back so I could make it back to the cabin, then to town. I had never felt this alone in my entire life. I had never been this afraid. I would not give in to tears. They would only help drain me of water. I needed that also. I tried not to think of a hot shower to wash his stink from me. My lip hurt from the first strike and was swollen.

I closed my eyes and pulled myself up into a ball. I held myself and tried to keep what heat there was in the sleeping bag inside. I would survive, somehow.

24

Montana

I woke feeling dirty, bloody, and exhausted. The sun was barely up. I looked at my watch, but the crystal face was broken, the hands not moving. I stared at it, trying to recall when or how I had broken my lovely watch. A beautiful watch that John had given me so long ago. Now it was broken. "It can be fixed," I wished.

As I tried to sit up, I realized that every muscle in my body was aching. I felt like someone had taken a baseball bat to me during the night. The taste of blood was still in my mouth. Slowly, I removed the sleeping bag from around my tattered body and found my boots that were still at the foot of the sleeping bag by the side of the tent wall. Reaching for them, I wanted to cry out as hot pain soared through the center of my body and down my legs.

I finally got my boots on, opened the tent flap, and made an attempt to stand. I was determined to not show Michael that I was in a great deal of pain. Looking around, he was nowhere to be seen. The campfire was flickering as it had not burned down completely. Walking over to the fire, I noticed one water bottle left out and the smaller backpack that I had been carrying. Jake's folding water dish was gone, the larger backpack was gone and no dinner dishes were left out. The site had been cleaned up as if I had been the only person there.

I painfully walked over, picked up the water bottle, took in a mouth full, and rinsed my mouth out. I spit the bloody water out and then took a few smaller drinks. Fear was taking over as the full aspect of my situation started sinking into my dull brain. I also realized my head was hurting. "Jesus, is there anything on me that's not hurting?"

I sat down on a flat rock near the fire, trying to control my breathing so that I would not fly into a full panic. "You bastard! You're ashamed of what you have done to me so you just leave me out here in the middle of nowhere? I guess you are hoping I don't make it back. I got news for you: I'm not only going to make it back, I'm going to put your ass in jail." Talking out loud made me feel tougher and not so afraid. Also I was still in bear country so I had better keep up the noise so I didn't startle any bears. I looked down at my hands, finding what appeared to be skin and some blood under my nails. I couldn't help but smile as I realized I did hurt him after all. Then I wondered why he hadn't bothered to just go ahead and kill me. Was he playing some sort of game? Was the rape a one-time thing? No; he had said something about the others.

I pulled myself off the rock, deciding I needed to see what he had left me to survive on. Picking up my pack, I found the same things I had before. My jacket, a pair of jeans, a pair of socks, and a water bottle. That gave me two water bottles, but only one was full. "Matches. Where are my matches?" I rifled through every pocket in and outside of the pack and found a book of matches with only a couple of matches inside. I checked my pockets. "Where is the box of matches I had?"

I pulled the tent door flap open and noticed for the first time there was only one sleeping bag left in the tent. "Bastard took his sleeping bag! Okay, calm down. What do you need with two sleeping bags? It would only be more weight to carry!"

I grabbed my sleeping bag, pulling it out of the tent and shook it. My box of matches fell to the ground and I heard a big breath of relief leave me body. I picked them up and tucked them into my jeans pocket. Something shinny caught my attention. It was my cell phone! I had forgotten I had stuffed it into my pocket. I picked it up and turned it on. Of course there was no cell signal, so I powered it back down. No sense in wasting what power it had. Now all I had to do was walk until I found a signal and I could call for help. It was then I noticed how dirty and bloody I was. "Ya don't need to be stomping around in the woods with bloody clothes on girl." I took my boots off, peeled off my pants, wished I had clean underwear to put on but I didn't, so I took the dirty, bloody ones off and folded them up with the pants. I didn't have another T-shirt so I would maybe wash this one out later. I retrieved my jeans from the pack, along with the clean socks, and carefully put them on and my boots. Just that little bit of clean clothing made me feel somewhat better. But, I could still smell the rape on my body.

I folded and rolled the sleeping bag, preparing it to be packed. Then I took down the tent, folding and rolling it up, ready to be packed away. With that done, I noticed some of the stiffness in my muscles was subsiding a bit, but certain ways I moved caused sharp pains to shoot from my crotch upward into my belly. I looked at the soiled pants and underwear, trying to decide what to do. Finally, I tossed them into what remained of the fire. After they were reduced to ashes, I started kicking dirt onto the remaining hot coals. I wasn't going to waste any water that I still had to douse the small fire.

"Okay, girl, now what?" I took a seat on top of the backpack as it felt softer on my sore backside than sitting on the flat rock again. "Assess the situation. Make a plan. Do what you know. This isn't helping much. The situation is that I'm totally lost, totally alone, and I have no food!"

I sat there for a few more minutes, trying to think positive. "Okay, Michael said this was the way to another trail that cut back toward the cabin. So there is no sense in trying to back track. I couldn't track our steps over all those rocks, anyway. If I keep going in the direction we were going and make my way until I find water, then I can follow the water."

I stood, looking around, trying to shake the creepy feeling that someone was watching me. Maybe this was just a test. Maybe Michael was playing some kind of sick joke, trying to see how I would react to being left alone in the middle of nowhere. Then it came to me that Jake didn't know how to play sick games. I whistled as loud as I could, and then yelled, "Jake! Here Jake!" I stood still, listening, but I heard nothing. Nothing but my own breath, the wind in the trees below me and maybe the faint sound of water falling in the distance. No Jake bounding his way toward me from afar. "Who are you kidding? You're out here alone! Deal with it!"

I grabbed my pack and swung it up into place on my back. It was very light so there was no problem other than my sore muscles and the strap landing on top of the bite wound. I had looked earlier and what little I could see it didn't look like it was getting infected. I wondered how long I could stand the strap from the backpack rubbing the wound. Turning so the sun was over my right shoulder, I started walking. Just a few feet beyond the flat clearing the land crumbled into fist size white rocks, falling into nothingness below me. One false step and I would be going with them. I slowly made my way along the top of the ridge. I realized I was being way too quiet and was likely to walk up on a grizzly so I started singing. I can't carry a tune in a bushel basket as my mom used to say, so my singing would scare off anything that wanted to do me harm. "Maybe you should have sung to Michael the other night. That's not even funny!" I kept trying to sing and still pay attention to where I placed each step.

After what seemed like hours, I finally started descending down off the ridge top. The hiking was easier as I had finally run out of the loose rocks. I was now back into some trees and even over the sound of the wind blowing through the pines I could hear water. I felt a new spark of relief. Still singing and watching each step, I finally made it to what appeared to be the bottom of a gulch with a small mountain creek. I pulled my water bottle from my pack and took a long drink. "This is a nice spot to camp." I looked around and realized I should fill my bottles and move on.

"It will be cold down here in this bottom. You need to climb."

Looking around, I tried to determine where the sun was and in which direction I should be walking. "Follow the water! OK, good idea, but it's getting late. Find a place to camp."

Looking across the little creek, I could see a game trail leading up the side of the gulch. "It would be better to find a clearing to camp tonight and stay out of this thick area and away from the water. Critters of the night might come here to drink." So, I started walking up the trail. What I thought was about a half hour, I came to a good size flat place up out of the tree line. Rocky, but a good place to spend the night. I was tired, sore, hungry, and scared. I looked at the sun and figured I had a couple of hours before it would be completely dark. I set my pack on a large flat boulder and unpacked the tent. I stood with the sun on my left and turned just a bit to my right. I figured this time of the year and this far North the sun would be setting in the Northwest. My tent door would be facing north when I woke in the morning. I made short time of erecting the tent and stretching the sleeping bag out inside.

"Okay, now get some fire wood and a fire going." I reached into the pack and pulled out my jacket. I zipped it halfway up and jammed my hands into the pockets. To my surprise, both pockets held treasures. I pulled out a protein bar from one and my small pocket knife from the other. I had totally forgotten I had stuck them in my jacket the other day. "Okay, we now have dinner! First things first, fire!"

I put the protein bar back in my pocket and stuck the knife in my jeans pocket. With that happy thought, I started gathering small twigs, then larger limbs. It didn't take me long to gather a good size stack of fire makings. I then gathered some large rocks, placing them in a circle to make a fairly large fire pit. Within minutes, I was warming myself next to a nice campfire in plenty of time before the night settled in on me. I was so hungry I thought about gobbling the protein bar down in several bites, but instead I broke off half, wrapped the left over half up in the paper, and put it back in my jacket pocket. "Bears. Better stick that food someplace else, dumb ass." I pulled the bar out of the pocket and placed it in the backpack that was resting on a rock near the edge of the other side of the clearing. "Better safe than sorry."

I took my time with the half of protein bar. Taking small bites, chewing it until there was just mush in my mouth, and then chasing it down with small sips of water. "I wonder what's in the water. Some kind of Montana germ, no doubt!" I laughed to myself. The last thing I needed was dysentery. "I wonder which is worse, dying from dysentery or being eaten by a bear?"

After eating, I found a place to relieve myself. My lady parts were still not happy and the pain returned as I stood from my squat. I sucked in a long breath as I arranged my clothing. I opened the tent flap and crawled in. The sun was down and I only had the glow of dusk and the light from the fire. "You going to take your boots off? Nope, I don't think so. I might need to make a daring escape." With that decision made, I settled into the sleeping bag, jacket, clothes, and boots still on. My pocket knife was in my front jeans pocket where I could get to it in a hurry.

Again, the feeling that someone was watching my campsite crept over me. "Stop freaking yourself out! There's no one out here but me and the critters. The critters are more afraid of me than I am of them. I doubt that!" I realized it wasn't just my lady parts that were still sore from the attack the night before, but my whole body ached. What would I give for a couple of *Aleve*? I was thankful for being exhausted and I soon fell into a deep sleep. If something or someone wanted to do me harm, I would probably sleep through most of it.

25

Montana

I woke with a jolt. I tried not to jump. It took everything I had to lie there trying to get my bearings. It was barely daylight. What had awakened me? I strained to hear anything that would give me a clue, but all I could hear was the bit of wind blowing through the pines below the ridge.

As quietly as I could, I unzipped the sleeping bag and folded it away from my feet. I sat up with less pain than the day before. "That's good," I whispered to myself. I slowly got to my hands and knees and moved the tent flap so that I could see the clearing. I didn't see anything or anyone, so I stepped out of the tent and stood. "Still sore but better. Today should be an easier day."

Looking at the fire, fear ran through me, almost knocking me to the ground. I realized I had not been alone. The fire was still smoldering from the night before, but someone had rearranged the rocks I had circled to make the fire pit. Panic was setting in and the thought of running off into the woods like a fool was sounding like a good idea in the back of my mind. Instead, I casually looked around while I walked over to the newly arranged rocks. Pretending as if I hadn't noticed, I picked up a couple of small sticks and stirred the ash covered coals. "Guess I better get going." I turned and walked back to the tent.

I folded the sleeping bag and tent. I packed them away into my backpack. I kept my jacket on as it was still chilly. I had no idea what the temperature was and I really didn't care. I just needed to move on. I got my pack up on my back and then took the time to look around. "Oh crap! The fire!"

I let the pack fall as I walked over to the fire. I started kicking what dirt I could find on the coals. "Don't need to start a forest fire on top of everything else," I chastised myself. The fire was still hot, so even though it was beyond my better judgment, I took one of the water bottles and sprinkled the fire with all of the water. That left me what was left in the other bottle. As soon as I made my way back down to the creek I passed last night, I would have two full bottles again. With that thought, I took out the other bottle and took a big drink. I tucked the bottle back into the backpack, and then swung it back onto my shoulders. The bite wound sent a shot of pain down my arm. "Please do not let that get infected," I said to no one there.

Looking around, I decided it would be easier to hike forward and downward than to back track to the water. I could still hear it below me. I figured that was a good sign. "What day is it?"

"It's Saturday. Why?" came Michael's voice from the far side the clearing.

I turned with such speed, I almost fell over. I felt fear stab me in the middle of my stomach. "Did you come back to finish me off? Bet you are surprised to see me still alive!" Without looking at him directly in the eye, I turned back around and started walking toward the edge of the clearing.

"Naw. I've been watching you all along. Did you like my handy work with the rocks?"

"I didn't pay any attention. What rocks?" I didn't look, but I could tell he was gaining on me. I tried to step up my pace, but again I found myself in loose rocks. About that time Jake went flying past me, tail wagging, having a grand time. He never looked back. He was out of sight in a few seconds. "Well, Jake is having a great time."

"You aren't?" Michael was right behind me.

I stopped and turned around, looking him square in the eyes. "What kind of game are you playing with me, Michael? You enjoy watching people trying to find their way? What kind of sick bastard are you, anyway?"

"Well, if you feel that way, maybe I should just leave you to yourself. Find your own way back!"

"I thought you left me out here to do that, anyway. If that's not the case, then just take me back to town. I need to get home."

"Why? I thought you liked it out here in the middle of nowhere." Michael reached for me, but I jerked away, out of his reach. Only this time I did lose my balance and stumbled backward. I slid down the side of the ridge a few feet on my butt, my pack protecting my back. I was grabbing for anything I could grab to stop my fall. I could feel my fingernails breaking and tearing. Finally, I stopped up against a large bolder about half my size. I had scrapes and scratches all over my hands

181

and arms. I just laid there for a few minutes trying to catch my breath.

I finally looked around and saw that I was alone again. No sign of Michael or Jake. I slowed my breathing so that I could hear better. Again, there was just the sound of the wind in the pines and the creek below me. I looked up toward the top of the ridge and, to my surprise, I had covered more area than I thought. I was a good twenty feet from where I had been standing. I finally got my feet under me and stood. "That was graceful! What else can you do for entertainment?" Looking over the top of the bolder, I couldn't see the bottom of the gulch. I decided I needed to keep moving parallel to the top of the ridge while looking for a better way to the bottom.

I had no way of knowing how long I had been hiking as the tall pines were blocking out most of the sun. I thought I was moving northeast, but being honest with myself I really had no clue. I kept trying to make as much noise as I could, talking and singing so I wouldn't surprise any bears. "No bear in its right mind would be walking around here." I laughed to myself.

I found a little clearing and decided to stop and take a rest. I had water, but was really wishing I had something to eat. "Don't think about food. It will only make you hungrier." I took several small drinks, trying to conserve what water I did have. Before I knew what was happening, I felt tears running down my cheeks. "Crap! Don't start crying! What good will that do?" But the tears came. I felt broken. Defeated. I was in no man's land, not knowing where in the hell I was or where I was going. As far as I knew, the man I thought was a decent guy was some kind of lunatic. I rubbed my checks with my dirty hands and wiped my nose on my jacket sleeve. I was a mess. I rubbed my hand through my nasty chopped up hair. Anger flooded through me. "You Asshole! You haven't won yet!" My words echoing off rocks made me feel even more alone. On the other hand, maybe someone would hear me, I thought on a wish and a prayer.

I put my water bottle away and started walking again. Soon I found myself on the top of the ridge, above the trees. I stopped and looked around. I was fairly high up, but not as high as other mountain tops around me. I could not see any trails or bodies of water. Just rocks and trees. "Crap, I'm tired of rocks and trees." I did notice that the ridge looked as if it was dropping away from me. If I could walk along the top of the ridge, following it down into the bottom of the gulch, maybe I would finally come across that creek again. I didn't even know if this was a good plan. "Face it, Dawn; you have no clue as to what you are doing."

The sun was getting lower in the sky much faster than I had hoped. Which only meant another night outside. I could already feel the air cooling. "Okay, if I walk until the sun goes down, I will still have enough light to make camp and build a fire. There's a plan!" With that decision, I started along the ridge top. I walked for maybe a half mile, give or take a few hundred feet when I came to a stop. I was facing a large rock slide. I looked over the edge of the ridge and all I could see was loose rocks. I could barely make out the creek at the very bottom. Right below me was a ledge and I could see the bottom of the gulch. I was either going to go down the slide to the bottom or try and go across the slide. It was getting too late to start off in either direction. I decided to make camp and spend the night right where I was and face the loose rocks tomorrow after I had rested.

I back tracked just a bit so that I could gather some firewood from the tree line just below me. I didn't have enough flat ground to set up the tent. I found a place near the rock slide to spread out the tent still folded in half. Then I placed my sleeping bag between the halves. The bottom half would serve as insulation from the cold, hard ground and the upper half would keep any moisture off my bag and help keep the heat inside. It was the best idea I could come up with.

I got the fire started in no time at all. "Still the fire starter, huh, John?" I wasn't sure why he had popped into my mind. Being honest with myself, I knew he was always there, someplace, lurking around in my memory. I wanted to blame John! If you hadn't decided you didn't want to be married, none of this would be happening. "Can't blame John. You're the one that wouldn't give him another chance. You're the one that told him no. You're the one that made the trip out here looking for Mr. Perfect. Dumb ass! Maybe John was as perfect as they get?"

I sat by the fire as I ate the last half of the protein bar. It was dry and hard, but it still tasted excellent. I tried to make it last as long as possible. I finished, stuck the wrapper in the pack, saving it for fire starter later. With my body warmed from the fire, I crawled into the sleeping bag, zipped the sides up, and pulled the tent over my body. "I really am getting too old for this sleeping on the ground crap." Exhaustion replaced any fear that was hanging over me.

26

Montana

From a short distance away, Michael sat on his backpack enjoying some dried fruit as he watched her build her fire. It looked like she was eating something, but from this distance he wasn't sure. "Wonder what she could be eating, Jake?"

Jake looked at him as he finished what little kibble Michael had given him. Then he laid down next to his fold up bowl.

As Michael watched her climb into her sleeping bag, his thoughts went to the other night. How surprised she had been when he lost his gentle touch and showed her how a real man takes a woman. He could feel the burn starting. He rubbed at his crotch and smiled. "That brings back a few good memories. I bet your John never gave it to you like you needed."

He tried to remember the first time, so many years ago. Hold old was he really? Was he fourteen like he had said? He thought so. It had been with his older second cousin. She was sixteen and wanted to lose her virginity. She had decided to teach her younger cousin how to kiss and during the lesson she reached down to find him hard as a rock.

"You're quite the man, aren't you, Mikey?" She laughed as she took his hand and allowed him to feel her breast. "First time you ever touched a titty, huh?" She laughed some more.

"I could show you how much of a man I am!" He pushed her onto her back and quickly got on top of her. He could see the smirk on her face, which pissed him off. "You don't think I can, do you?"

She shoved him off her. Getting to her feet, she decided it was time for both of them. He didn't know she was a virgin and he probably didn't know the difference. She slowly took her blouse off, then her shorts. She was standing in her panties and bra and he could only stare. She let her bra drop to the ground. Hooking her thumbs into her bikini panties, she slid them down and stepped out of them.

As she laid down on the old back seat of a junked car in her daddy's back yard, Mikey tore at his clothing. Standing naked, she eyeballed his erection. "Come on, Mikey. Do me."

He almost pounced on top of her. Between her legs, he fumbled to find the right spot. She took him into her hand and guided him. She winced as he pushed into her and with his second push it was over.

"Really?" She mocked. "Is that it?" She pushed him away.

Embarrassed, he grabbed his clothes and headed to the back of the garage, leaving her there wet and naked. Mikey could still hear her laughing.

"Well, that was a long time ago. All that practicing I did with daddy's Playboys sure made a difference a couple of years later, didn't it, Jake?" Michael, deep in thought, rubbed his crotch again. Jake was sound asleep. Michael turned back to more old memories.

Two years later, Mikey was driving an old beat up *Ford* that had seen its better days. He didn't care. It got him where he wanted to go and the backseat proved to be a love nest for the girls in his class that would let him have his way with them.

Then it happened one day. He saw his cousin standing on the corner by the city's only drug store. He stopped the *Ford* and leaned across the bench seat, yelled out of the window, "Hey, you need a ride there, cous?"

"Sure. I don't feel like walking home in this heat. It's not even summer yet and already it's too hot to do anything." She slid into the front seat, shut the door, and didn't bother to pull her too short skirt down.

Michael pulled up into the driveway and shut the engine off. "Got anything cold to drink?"

Never thinking anything about the house being empty, her mom and dad at work, she guided Mikey into the kitchen. He followed behind her, watching her backside pushing against the skirt. "Your ass looks like puppies trying to get out of a croaker sack." He laughed.

Ignoring her cousin's rude remark, she threw her purse on the kitchen table as she walked over to the cupboard that held the iced tea glasses. She didn't know it, but Michael was already fully erect and had unzipped his jeans. As she reached for the cupboard door, he grabbed her, pushing her over and bending her at the waist. She tried to pull away, but he grabbed the back of her hair and held her in place with one hand as he pushed her skirt up to her waist.

"Fucker! Stop it!" But yelling wasn't going to stop him and there was no one to hear her. Before she could say another word, he ripped her panties from her body, spread her legs, and thrust himself into her.

"This won't be fast like the last time," he sneered. "I've had all sorts of practice."

The more she tried to pull away, the harder his grip became. She could feel hair being pulled from her scalp. She could feel her body tearing from his abuse. Tears ran down her cheeks, but she refused to scream. "Fuck you," she whispered.

"No, fuck you," he said. He not only raped her there in the kitchen, he then pulled her into the living room where he threw her onto the sofa. Still holding the back of her head, he mounted her and began again. She tried to twist away, which only fueled his rage. Mikey was biting her every place he thought the marks would not show if she was dressed. After he finished with her, he walked back into the kitchen. He took a kitchen towel from the counter, cleaned himself, threw the towel on the floor, and dressed.

"Ya better throw that towel away. Wouldn't want your whore mother smelling our loving."

She didn't move until she heard the *Ford* driving away.

About three months later, he heard his lovely dear cousin had moved away, in trouble with a bastard child. Mikey figured it was his bastard child and laughed at the thought.

Sitting there on the backpack, he lost control with the memories of that hot southern afternoon so long ago. It didn't take him long to find that old self-abuse pleasure. *Yep, I still got it,* he thought as he tucked himself back into his jeans.

"Tomorrow, Dawn. I'll give it to you again. You just wait."

27

Virginia

"Hello, John? This is Cindy." She was walking from the United Airlines customer service counter.

"Yeah, Cindy. She with you?"

"No, John. I waited until all the passengers had come down the hallway. I didn't see her. I thought I might have missed her so I came to baggage claims. She wasn't here either. When the last bag was picked up and I was the only one standing there, I went to customer service. She was not on the plane. They checked the Great Falls flight into Salt Lake and she wasn't on that flight either." Cindy was trying not to panic, but tears started building in her eyes.

"Cindy, calm down. It could be she just missed her flight. Did you try and call her?"

"Yes, I tried to call her early this morning. It went straight to her voice mail. It was five this morning, Montana time. Her flight was supposed to take off at six. She should have answered!"

"Cindy, you know how many times we have called and she let her phone battery die. That would be just like her. There really isn't much we can do for twenty four hours." Looking at his watch, he figured he could start calling authorities early the next morning.

"Twenty four hours? So you think she's really missing?" The tears over flowed onto her cheeks.

"I don't know. Just go home and once her phones charges she will call. She's probably stuck at the airport waiting on another flight. Don't worry until it's time to worry." Sounded good as the words were running over his lips, but it wasn't so easily done. Fear was creeping up into his throat. He knew he was right. Even if he called the Great Falls police, they wouldn't do much since it had only been a few hours.

John settled into the chair at the kitchen table at the little apartment he had rented in Richmond. His laptop came to life. He Googled Montana maps.

28

Montana

It's always the coldest just before dawn so goes the saying and this morning found me shaking from the cold. I tried to curl into a ball, holding what heat I had left in my core, but it was useless. I finally threw the tent from the top of me and unzipped the sleeping bag. I could see my breath as I let the air escape from my mouth.

"I need heat." As I stepped over to the smoldering left over campfire, I picked up a few small sticks and laid them on top of the coals. I gently blew on the ambers. "Ah ha, flames!" Quickly, I grabbed what few larger branches I had gathered the evening before and placed them on the smaller pile of sticks. Within minutes, the heat was rising. I stood as close as possible, while I rubbed my hands together to generate more heat. The warmth felt good enough that I forgot how empty my stomach was and the growling noises it was making.

I pulled the backpack up and sat on top of it next to the fire. I would wait there until the sun came up, when I could start my trek across the loose rocks and then down to the stream. As I set there soaking up the heat, I realized my body was healing. I could actually sit and rise without too much pain this morning. Once I was good and warm, I ventured near where I had slept and relieved myself. It was then I realized just how stinky I was and how badly I needed a bath.

"Stay smart. Even if you don't make it out of here alive, if anyone finds your body there will still be DNA. Don't you dare wash yourself! Silly girl, where in the hell are you going to wash? I would freeze to death in one of these mountain run off streams."

I picked up the tent, folded it, rolled it up, and stuffed it into the pack. That gave me even more cushion as I sat back down. I had a little while more to enjoy my fire before it was light enough to make my way safely. I wondered where Michael and Jake had spent the night. No doubt, probably not far from me. I was trying to ready myself for when he showed himself again.

"Good morning. Rest well?" Michael was just a few feet to my left.

Although it startled me, I didn't allow myself to jump up or even turn my head in his direction. "Good morning. Yes I did, as a matter of fact. And you?"

"Jake and I had an entertaining evening. Wish you would have joined us." I didn't look, but I knew he had that smirk of a smile on his face.

"You knew where I was; you could have joined me." I eased my hand down over my pocket to feel my little pocket knife. It gave me a little sense of safety, although I knew I had no chance in a knife fight. I just wasn't skilled enough in defense with a knife.

I stood and grabbed my pack, swinging it up onto my shoulders. The bite was hurting even more than it was yesterday and I wondered how much of my shoulder was infected. I didn't need that on top

194

of everything else, but the pain let me know it was indeed there.

"Going somewhere? Do you even know what direction you need to be heading?" He was now laughing.

"Any place you are not is a good place. How about we just part as friends?" I didn't even stop to kick dirt and rocks on what was left of the fire. If the wind picked up and sparks caught the forest on fire, so be it. Maybe fire fighters would come to fight the blaze and someone would find me or my body.

I was about twenty feet from the fire, about half way out onto the rock slide, carefully watching each step. I could feel his eyes on my back. Just past what I thought was the halfway mark, I reached a flat rock. I was surrounded by the rocks from the slide. I stopped and turned to see Michael about four feet away. Jake was nowhere in sight.

I turned to step off the rock when Michael grabbed my right arm. "Hey, let's say we kiss and make up?"

"You really are an ass! I'm done, just leave me alone. Leave me here to die for all I care, just leave!" I jerked and tried to pull free. Michael let go of me and the force of my turn threw me off balance. What little weight I had in my back started pulling me backward off the rock. I was reaching for air. Panic in my eyes and throat.

For whatever reason, Michael grabbed at me. He caught me by the front of my jacket, pulling me back upright. As I regained my balance, I stepped behind him. I turned and pushed him as hard as I could in the middle of his pack. His body started to tilt forward. In a split second, I could see he was trying to turn to grab back hold of me. Again I shoved at him, only lower toward his hips. This knocked him off the rock as he lost his center of gravity. Instead of fighting the fall, he seemed to tuck his head into a somersault. Only it didn't work. The weight of the pack only exaggerated the flip.

I watched as he flipped over and over down the loose rocks. He yelled at first and then there were just grunts. He lost his cap and the pack about half way down the slope. On one of the flips, I thought I heard a leg bone snap. I dismissed the thought, thinking there was too much noise for me to hear a bone breaking.

I was frozen to the rock watching Michael fall away from me. What seemed like minutes was actually only a few seconds. He finally stopped with his backpack stopping twenty feet sooner. It was then I realized his leg had snapped. He had stopped on his back with his arms splayed to each side. His left leg was bent at the knee and his foot at a very slight angle. The right leg was spread in the other direction. However, halfway between his knee and his ankle the leg turned at a right angle. His right foot faced the wrong way. I was too far away to see if he was still breathing.

I took my pack from my shoulders, sat it on the flat rock, and sat down. "Access the situation," I said to myself, but all I wanted to do was fly away. Fly back to town. Fly back to Richmond. "Crap, what day is it?" I thought it might be Sunday, but I wasn't sure.

"If it's Sunday, someone will be looking for me. Cindy should be calling." I pulled my cell phone from my pocket and turned it on. Still no signal. I shut it back off.

There was still no noise from Michael. "Should I go down there and see if the bastard is still alive? Why? After what he did to me? Let him rot!" I thought about it for a few more minutes and decided even if he was alive there was no way I could get him off the mountain. I was not strong enough to carry or even support a man his size. His leg was broken and useless. The best thing I could do would be find my way out, find either the cabin or someone else. I knew there were fishing streams and campgrounds in the area. I just didn't know in what direction. Just how big was the Lewis and Clark Forrest, anyway? Being honest with myself, I really didn't know if I was actually in the Lewis and Clark Forrest. I did remember seeing something about Sun Canyon and Benchmark, but I couldn't remember where or when.

I stood, grabbed my pack, and hoisted it up onto my back again. Michael was right. I was getting better with practice. Slowly, as not to step on the wrong rock sending me to the bottom where his body laid, I took my time making it to the far edge of the slide. Just as I made it off the rocks, I heard a moan.

"Stop. Don't leave me here like this!" Michael's plea came from below.

"I can't help you. Your leg is broken. I can't carry you." I didn't want to turn to look at him, but I did. I could see the pain and fear in his eyes.

"When I catch up with you, you're dead if you leave me here like this!" He was trying to scream.

"You were going to leave me to die, anyway! I'm going for help. I need your DNA to prove what you did to me and probably others." I turned and started walking into the sparsely wooded area.

"Come back here! Bitch! You're gonna die!" came the screams from the broken man in the rocks.

I didn't look back and the further I walked, the weaker his screams became.

29

Virginia

Sunday morning at six, John had already called Cindy. She had tried calling Dawn during the evening, several times during the night, and just minutes ago. He only admitted to calling Dawn's cell a few times. Still there was nothing but voice mail. John and Cindy both had a terrible sinking feeling that neither one could shake.

Ted was in D.C working the whole weekend, leaving Cindy plenty of time alone to go into full panic mode. She was on her way over to John's place. She couldn't stay still any longer.

John heard her pull up into the drive. She was knocking on the door even before he could make his way across the living room to open the door for her.

"Come in. I'm about to call the Great Falls Police." He led her to the little kitchen where they both took a seat at the table.

Cindy looked at the scattered papers with notes jotted in different directions. There were also maps of Montana that John had printed off from the computer. There were phone numbers jotted here and there with names next to the numbers. She tried to piece together the notes with no success.

***

"Yes, my name is John Hinds. I'm calling from Richmond, Virginia. I'm calling to report a

199

possible missing person." John was using his best police voice.

"Just a moment, sir. I'll connect you with one of our detectives," the dispatcher said politely.

"Officer Wilson."

"Officer Wilson, this is John Hinds. I'm calling from Richmond, Virginia. I would like to report a possible missing person."

"Why possible?" Wilson asked.

"My wife was on vacation in your area and was to fly home yesterday. She never arrived home. She never checked in for her flight. We have been calling for several days and her cell phone goes straight to voice mail."

"Well, Mr. Hinds, lots of wives forget to charge their cell phones. And for that matter, lots of wives go on trips and decide they don't want to go back home. Happens all the time."

"Look, I'm also a cop. Okay, I *was* a cop. I just took an early retirement from a city police department in Alabama. I know the routine. Something just isn't right. Dawn is very responsible and she has a job here. If she was upset with me, she would still call her friends and let them know why she wasn't on the flight." John was trying not to let his frustration leak into his comments.

"Is your wife upset with you?" Wilson asked.

"Okay, here's the deal. We are separated. Dawn thought we were divorced, but the

200

final papers never went through. In the meantime, she started communicating with some guy on a dating site. She flew to Great Falls to meet this guy and spend time with him over in Augusta. I called you first since she flew into Great Falls and was supposed to fly out of there. The thing is, it's not just me that is concerned, but her friends are worried also."

"Do any of you know the person she is supposed to have met up with over in Augusta?" Wilson wasn't sounding too interested. Another love triangle turned sour, he likely thought.

"That's just the point. After talking with her friends here in Richmond about her trip, I did some investigating on my own regarding this guy. The person he claims to be, a Michael Conrad, a gunsmith according to his website. But I have come to learn that Michael Conrad actually died in a car crash several years ago."

Wilson was now showing a little interest. "You have verified all of this information, Hinds?"

"Yes. I talked to the Police Chief in Idaho Falls. He sent me the coroner's report. The real Michael Conrad is dead, broken neck in a crash going home from a gun show in Jackson Hole, Wyoming."

"I see. Well, there are no city police in Augusta. The Lewis and Clark sheriff's department takes care of any problems there. Augusta is a small community, everyone knows everyone. The only problems that arise there, is during the annual rodeo, mostly DUIs and drunken fights. I'll give Sheriff Burk a call and see if he can have one of his deputies check things out. You have an address for this Conrad guy?

"No; all we have is Augusta." John and Wilson exchanged cell phone numbers and he gave Wilson Cindy's numbers. Wilson agreed to call back as soon as he heard anything from the deputy.

John sat looking at the cell phone after the call was ended. "Come on, Dawn, call one of us!" he demanded.

Cindy's face was a ball of fear. "You think he will do what he says?"

"All we can do is wait and see." John wasn't good at waiting, but there was nothing else he could do except keep searching the web. "Cindy, what is the name of that web site?"

"MrPerfect.com. Why; you think you can find something there?" There was a flicker of hope in her question.

"Maybe. I just want to get a look at this so called Conrad."

Cindy grabbed the laptop and slid it in front of her. "Here, let me. I know the site and Dawn's password if she didn't change it. I set this up for her." Tears starting building up in her eyes. "This is my fault."

"Don't go there again. We can all take part of the blame later. After we find her." John stood and stepped behind Cindy so he could see what she was doing.

Cindy got into Dawn's account. There was a new photo of her that John hadn't seen before. One taken in her apartment in Richmond. He couldn't help but notice she was just as beautiful as ever. The years were being good to her.

"John, I don't think you should read the comments between them. I can get to his profile and that's really what you want, isn't it?" Cindy quickly typed on the keyboard and within seconds there he was, Michael Conrad.

John stared at the computer screen. "Well, that's the face which pulls up when you Google Michael Conrad or you look into the gunsmith web site." Reaching across the table, John opened a folder and pulled out several pieces of paper. "This is Michael Conrad's Idaho driver's license the coroner attached to the autopsy report."

Cindy took the photo from his hands, looked at it, and then at the computer screen. "Oh my god! John, these are two different men! Which one is the real Michael?"

"I don't even want to say this, but I would bet that the real Michael is in the cemetery in Idaho Falls. Our problem is, who in the hell is Dawn with right now and where is she?"

They spent the morning searching the Internet and reading the files John had received from the Idaho police department. With no lunch and too much coffee later, John started pacing. "If we don't hear anything by tomorrow, I'm going to fly to Great Falls. I can't stay here and do nothing!"

Cindy watched John as he started unpacking duffle bags and backpacks. He was sorting gear into several different piles. "What are you doing?"

"I'm trying to decide what I should take with me. There's a good chance this might turn into a mountain search and rescue and I want to be prepared."

"Search and rescue?" Tears were building in Cindy's eyes. "I want to go with you!"

"Cindy, I don't want to sound unkind, but having you along would only hinder any progress anyone would make. Your idea of hiking is walking around the mall and roughing it would be not doing lunch while you were at the mall."

"That's not fair, but probably truer than I want to admit. There has to be something I can do?" She fought back the tears.

"You can help me pack."

Cindy's phone rang at five, but it was Ted calling from D.C. "Any word?

"No; we are waiting for the Great Falls police to call. John is flying out tomorrow morning. I want to go, but he said no."

"He's right, Honey. I'm heading home in a few minutes. Screw work; I need to be there with you. I'll be home in a couple of hours. You going to be home or at John's"

"Call when you get to north Richmond and I'll let you know where I am. Drive safe."

Cindy had just ended the conversation when John's phone rang.

"Hinds here!" There was a desperate note in his voice.

"Mr. Hinds, the sheriff department just called and there is no record of a Michael Conrad in Augusta. There are several new residents, but no one seems to know who they are, if they are just summer renters or new year round residents. One neighbor said he has seen a tall man and a black lab from time to time, but has never really talked to the man. Said he's not very friendly and stays gone for days at a time. He said he thought the man was taking care of the house since the elderly woman living there might have gone to live with her kids down in Helena. That's about all we know."

"That isn't much help, Wilson. Do I need to be there to file the missing person's report?"

"No, let me get the forms. I'll take the information from you over the phone and get things into motion on this end."

"I have a reservation for a flight out in the morning. There is no easy way to get to Great Falls. The only way I could get there was from Minneapolis or from Salt Lake. I won't be there until late tomorrow afternoon."

"Do you want one of my officers to pick you up at the airport?"

"No; I have already rented a SUV. Thanks anyway."

It took about forty-five minutes for Wilson to take down all the needed information on Dawn; her flight plans and what little information John had on Conrad. John ended the call and flopped down on the sofa, feeling drained of every ounce of energy. Bowing his head, holding the sides of his skull, Cindy heard him mumble, "Please, God, don't let me lose her, even if she will not take me back."

Cindy softly said, "Amen."

30

Montana

After all that Michael had done to me, I was still fighting the guilty feeling of leaving another human in such a horrible situation. I still knew that I had to push on and find help. To save myself. I needed food. I was hungry.

After I made it off the rock slide, I started down another slope, not as steep but I still slowed my pace trying to be careful. Finally I made my way to the bottom and found a tiny run off trickle of a stream. I laid my pack on a large rock and found a little pool a bit deeper than the stream. I lowered myself onto my hands and knees, and then rocked back on my heels. I looked around me to make sure I was alone and then leaned forward, sticking my head into the cold mountain water. Taking my hands and rubbing my face until I couldn't hold my breath any longer, I pulled myself out of the water. I opened my eyes and, startled, I let out a scream. Inches from my face was Jake. "Cheese and Rice, Jake! You scared the crap out of me!"

Jake responded with a lick to my cheek and a fiercely wagging tail. My heart rate slowing. I laughed and petted the wet dog. The cold water from my head ran down into my T shirt and jacket. I decided I should pull the jacket off and save that warmth for later.

"Jake, I'm really hungry. I need to find something, anything. I bet you are getting hungry, too."

Jake stood there watching me as I filled my water bottles and packed them away. I slid into the back pack, wrenching as the straps hit my shoulder. "Jake, my body is feeling better but my shoulder still hurts like hell."

I stood there looking at the direction the water was flowing and decided that was the direction I should be going. "Come on, Jake; let's go this way."

Looking confused and looking back in the direction he had probably come, Jake just stood there as I crossed the small stream and started walking away. "Jake, come on, boy."

Jake didn't move. In fact, he sat down and gave a little whine. "Jake, I know you don't understand. Your daddy is kind to you, but he's a monster! We had to leave him. He's broken up. I have to try and find help for me and for him." I kept walking and talking.

I was well out of sight when Jake finally caught up with me. I was still walking along the small stream at the bottom of the gulch. I wondered how long it would be before I would find help or if I ever would. "Don't think like that! Follow the water! Follow the water!"

I walked along the bank, making my way around downed trees and sometimes over them. I was trying to be careful. The last thing I needed was another injury. Anything serious and I would end up like Michael. No one would ever know where our bodies lay. And what about Jake? What would happen to him?

"I guess you have given up on going back to save your daddy, huh boy?" Jake had not gotten out of my sight since he caught up with me a few hours ago. We walked a good ways, stopped to get a drink, and then carried on. At the last stop, I noticed I was feeling more weak and warm. More like a cold sweat. That might mean several things, but the thought of infection or blood poisoning seared through my thoughts. I finally stopped walking, sat the backpack down, and peeled my T-shirt off. I looked at my shoulder and saw the redness had worsened and had spread. It now was spreading down into my bicep. "Oh God! This is getting much worse." I reached down into the cold stream, collected some water, and placed my hand over the redness. The cool water felt good on the hot skin. "We have to speed up, boy. I have to get out of here before the infection takes completely over." I was between a rock and a hard spot. I needed to speed up to find help, but speeding up would cause my heart rate to increase, causing the infection to spread faster.

Jake and I started walking again when I noticed the stream seemed to be getting wider. *That might be a good sign,* I thought to myself. I was scanning the area around the stream when I got a glance of some purple berries. "Look Jake! Berries!"

It occurred to me that I wouldn't be the only one looking for something to eat. Bears love berries, too. I picked up a long stick, about five feet long and about four inches around. As I walked closer to the bushes, the more I struck the stick on the surrounding rocks, smaller trees, and bushes. I broke into 'Delta Dawn' as loud as I could sing. If

209

that didn't scare off everything in the area, then nothing would.

We finally made our way to the bushes that held a bounty of ripened berries. I found myself picking and pushing them into my mouth as fast as I could move. They were not as sweet as blueberries and were smaller. "These must be Huckleberries. These are probably the best berries I have ever eaten!"

Jake was giving me the big brown eyed stare. "Oh, sorry. Doggies eat berries, too?"

I held a handful of berries down for Jake to sniff. At first, I thought he was going to turn his nose up at the idea, but he finally ate a few. I found myself laughing. "Good boy."

We ate our full and I packed every pocket of the backpack full of berries. If we had nothing else, we had berries and water. Far more than I had this morning. I set off to find a place to camp for the night as it wouldn't be long before the sun sank behind the high mountain ridges to my left.

The berries had given me a little energy even though I was feeling feverish. Coming into a clearing, I gently laid the pack on the rocks so I wouldn't smash the berries. I looked for a place to place the tent, but again decided to place my back against a big rock, fold the tent in half, and nest myself between the layers. I was feeling too tired to even eat any more berries. I decided not to build a fire just in case Michael had recovered and was tracking me. I could live a night without a fire.

I left my clothes and boots on, folded my jacket into a pillow, and eased myself into the sleeping bag. I patted the top layer of my nest and called Jake over, "Come here, boy."

Jake happily joined me on the top of the layers and curled up into a ball. If anything came near, Jake would sound the alarm and he radiated body heat. I soon gave in to exhaustion.

31

Great Falls, Montana

The wheels touched down at the Great Falls International airport shortly after six p.m. John found it strange that the flight was completely full. He would have never thought there were that many things to see and do here. Having done some research of the area, he learned that Great Falls was once the hub of excitement for this part of Montana. Who would have thought that great entertainers had once played in the night clubs in Great Falls? Why, even President Kennedy had visited the city. It was also known at the time for its Air Force base and its missile fields. When he really thought about it, he hadn't really known anything about Great Falls before just a few days ago.

Waiting in the small baggage claim area, he noticed there were more backpacks and fishing equipment on the carrousel than he had ever seen in any airport. After a few minutes, he saw his pack and bag coming around to his feet. Grabbing his gear, he made his way toward the two car rental counters.

It didn't take him long to finish the paperwork and find his SUV. It was even a shorter time to find the *Holiday Inn Express* at the bottom of the airport hill. First exit off I-15, very handy. John checked into his room, grabbed his cell phone, and called Wilson.

"Wilson here," came a strong voice on the other end.

"Hey Wilson. John Hinds. Any word from anyone?"

"We have no word from your wife, sorry. We do have a search and rescue team rounded up. We will be going to Augusta early in the morning. I can pick you up about five for the drive over, if you wish."

"I'm at the *Holiday Inn Express*. How about I meet you here and I can follow you?"

"Good. See you at five." And Wilson clicked off.

Hungry but not feeling like eating, John found himself wondering how old Wilson was and how long he had been a cop. Did he have a wife? Children? "I wonder if you ever let your job consume you to the point you lost the most important thing in the world," he asked to no one there.

John lay there thinking of all the things he could have or should have done differently. How many times had Dawn reached out to him, wanting his attention, his company, and his affection? How many times had he turned her away, always making an excuse so he didn't have to open his feelings up to her? Why had he been that way with her?

John knew the very first time he had seen her, even though she wanted no relationship with anyone then or ever as she had said, that he would win her love. He remembered how he would spend all of his free time, which wasn't much, with her. How she made him laugh. How happy he felt when he was with her. Why had he let that slip away? When did he let that slip away?

"Damn ego! That is all it boils down to, us men and our damn egos!" Trying to think of something else, he remembered too well the case he had been working on. A drug trafficking case. A big case that was going to make his career. It might even get him a detective's slot in the small department. It was all falling together. Not only did he have the goods on the low end druggies, but he also had the bigger fish. The ones supplying the drugs out of California into the small Southern town. The more things happened, the more time he was spending away from Dawn. In the back of his mind, he had told himself it would be worth it because if all played out as planned, everyone in jail, he would get his promotion and they would have more time to spend with each other.

The first thing that happened was the crap with that silly dispatcher. Nothing had ever really happened with that girl, but the card on the windshield said differently in Dawn's eyes. Dawn never knew that he had returned that card to the girl and had told her to never ever call his house, his cell phone, or his wife again. Dawn never knew that she had gotten fired and had moved away, never to be heard of again.

No, she never knew because shortly after that was when the case broke wide open and John was working fifteen to eighteen hours a day. When John found out that the County Sheriff was involved in the drugs coming into the area, John left. He was getting death threats from some of the Sheriff's followers. Only the other members on the undercover operation knew for sure what was going on and John swore them to silence when it came to Dawn. They had to prove what the Sheriff was involved in and put him in jail. They had to keep families out of it. John was the only married member of the unit and the only one with much to lose.

Months later, Dawn had moved to Birmingham. What she didn't know was that she had moved not far from the undercover set up house and the woman she would see John with was an undercover agent from a drug task force unit.

It took longer for the different units to make their cases and bring the Sheriff to justice. John had made many enemies in the small town. Lots of cops related to the Sheriff that believed he should be fired and just let go. The DEA, FBI, and the other drugs task force units didn't believe that for one minute.

In the end, all the bad guys went to jail. Most of them never went to court, didn't pass go, didn't collect two hundred dollars, just went straight to jail. A bad thing to be an ex-cop and be in jail. Many of them were in solitary confinement in Federal prison because of the cross state line charges.

The loser in the matter was John. Even though he had started and finished a big case and bad guys were in jail, his old job at the small police department turned to shit. No one wanted to work with him because he had put their cousin, their wife's cousin, their brother, or brother-in-law in jail. The Chief refused to promote John to detective and in the long run gave him crappy shifts and only rookies to work with on dog calls or loud noise reports.

His folks had told him Dawn had moved to Virginia and even though he already knew that, he pretended like it was news to him. He never told anyone that he never signed the final divorce papers, as in the back of his mind he knew one day he would have a chance to win her back.

When Dad ended up back in the hospital and he finally got the nerve to tell Dawn the divorce wasn't final, it also gave him the courage to take an early retirement and move to Virginia.

Now he lie in a hotel room in Great Falls, Montana, praying that the love of his life was still alive and that all his fears would be cast away when they found her safe. "Just be safe."

***

John woke with a start, being in a strange room and a strange noise outside his door. He looked at the red numbers on the bedside clock. It read four a.m. He didn't remember falling asleep. He was still in the same clothes he had put on the day before to make his way halfway across the country. He still had his hiking boots on and his mouth felt like someone had hiked through it all night with Army boots.

He prepared the little hotel coffee pot to brew while he jumped in the shower. After a quick shave, tooth brushing, and dressing, he still had plenty of time for some terrible hotel room coffee before Wilson arrived.

To his surprise, the coffee wasn't all that bad. He checked his phone for any messages, but the message app was blank. That meant Cindy had

216

heard nothing nor did anyone else. He needed to eat.

Looking at his watch, he still had twenty minutes and he had seen a Smith's grocery store on the corner while driving to the hotel. The sign said open twenty-for hours. Grabbing his gear and the bad coffee, John made his way to the SUV. Making his way to Smith's, he noticed the McDonalds across the street, but it wasn't open yet.

As he walked into the grocery store, the first thing he smelled was fresh donuts. Old cop habits die slowly. When he made it back to the *Holiday Inn*, he was eating his second doughnut and drinking from a quart container of milk. He was about to get out of the SUV when a black and white SUV pulled up beside him. A forty something, graying at the temples officer smiled. Both men rolled down their windows.

"Did you bring enough of those for everyone one?" Wilson smiled.

"If everyone is just you and me for now, I did." John grabbed the box of donuts, opened his door, and stepped over to the SUV.

John slid into the passenger seat, shook hands with Wilson, and opened the box. "Sorry, I'm not sharing my milk."

"I have plenty of coffee. You hear anything during the night from your Virginia friends or from Dawn?" Wilson talked while he ate.

"No, nothing." John just looked straight ahead.

"Well, let's get this show on the road. We are meeting the Sheriff and his Search and Rescue people in Augusta. This early means you need to drive a little more cautiously—lots of deer out this time of day."

"I'm right behind you. About fifty miles?"

"About."

32

Montana

"Jesus, now I know how Michael Conrad felt when I broke his neck," Mikey Strongbow whispered. Sweat had soaked his clothing and the dried blood from his wounds had moistened, causing the blood stains to spread. He didn't know how long it had been since he passed out. He had watched as Dawn walked out of his sight at the top of the drop off. All his yelling and screaming on how he was going to kill her probably never reached her ears.

After lying there for a while trying to decipher how bad his injuries actually were, he decided to try and move. Cuts and bruises all over his body, some he could only feel under the clothing. His arms were not broken, but it felt like his shoulder was close to being separated. Neck and back seemed to be intact, so he decided to try and sit up.

Halfway into a sitting position, he could finally see his twisted and broken leg. The other leg seemed alright, but the ankle looked sprung not only because it was twisted at an odd angle but the pain was throbbing.

"Goddamn bitch! You broke my fucking leg!" He lay back down easily as to not thump the back of his head again on the rocks. He could feel the dry blood on the back of his neck from a cut on his head somewhere. "Think Mikey, think! Where's my knife? Where's my pack?"

Sitting up again, he looked around. His pack was halfway down the rock slide. It was still intact, but he could not see his knife anywhere. "If I could find some large sticks, I could make a splint out of them and my belt."

Still sitting, he reached down, grabbed his thigh and tried to straighten his leg. Red hot flames shot up his leg, up into his stomach, causing him to lose what little breakfast he had eaten. "Man up, pussy! Man up, fix this leg, and find that cunt!" With all the power he could muster, he held onto his leg to keep it stable while pushing with his other leg, causing his butt and hips to move backward. The pain from his sprained ankle was bearable, but as the broken leg started to straighten, the pain grew to the point where Mikey passed out.

He woke with the sun beating down on his face. Gaining enough will power to sit up again and look at his leg, he had to know if it had straightened at all or if all his effort was in vain. Looking at what once was a horrible bend in the wrong direction, he now saw a somewhat straighter leg. Still useless but straighter.

"Okay, Mikey, you can do this. You are going to drag yourself backward off this rock slide and under that brush behind you. You can do this! You can do this!"

He spent the afternoon dragging his broken body over the rocks a few feet at a time, then stopping to rest. Several times the pain was too much. Passing out from the white hot splinters of pain, he would awake not knowing how long he had been out. Each time we awoke, he could tell the sun was getting lower and the swelling in the broken leg had worsened and the sprained ankle was twice its normal size. The more strain on his weakened body, the more he would sweat. He also thought his body was fighting the injuries with the onset of a fever. He knew come sundown, wet with sweat, no fire to warm himself, no splint on that leg, and no way to reach his pack, his future was not looking so great.

"Who's kidding who? What future? You never had one. Not from the start. Things were going pretty good for you; a new name, new life, new everything, but, no, ya just couldn't stop, could you?" he chastised himself for whatever reason. He knew it never did a bit of good. He had really planned on stopping. Stop the raping and the killing. It was worse than being addicted to heroin or crack. "Well, in a way it is being addicted to crack, only not the kind you smoke." He laughed aloud, a spiking fever making him crazy. He had stopped for a while after he killed Conrad. He spent the biggest part of a year making a new life and identity for himself.

He had stayed near Cody, Wyoming after killing Conrad. He had taken that time to learn as much about guns and knives as he could from an old dude he had met in Cody. They had become friends. Old Bill, everyone called him Old Bill. For some reason, he had taken a liking to Mikey and took him in. "Like the son I never had," Old Bill had said one time.

Like the father I never had, Mikey had thought to himself.

While Mikey learned from Bill, he kept a low profile. He would go down to the Cody library and work on their computer. He spent hours

221

building a new website and a new life based on the real Michael Conrad. One day there was a young girl in the library working on a computer. He struck up a conversation with the young girl. She was on vacation with her parents, with no laptop, so she was at the library catching up with her friends in Montana.

It didn't take long for him to charm the young girl into telling him all about Montana. How they lived in Helena, but had family in Great Falls and Augusta. Her grandma still lived in Augusta. They hardly ever went anywhere but Great Falls or Augusta for vacation, but this year they came to Cody and tomorrow they were going to Yellowstone.

"You should go to Montana someday. There's a lot of wide open spaces to get lost in there," the young girl said before she left.

"I just might do that one day," he said. Thinking for the first time in his life, while watching a young girl walk away from him, he was not aroused. Now Mikey lay in some bushes next to a rock slide in the middle of some wide open space, with no one around to hear him crying from the horrible pain in his legs. If he could survive the night, maybe tomorrow he could splint this leg and get back to the cabin. "That city bitch will not make it out of here. She's too stupid to find any kind of trail, much less back to the cabin or Augusta."

He tried not to think about the pain, the cold, or the blood. If he had any luck at all there would be no bears or wolves to deal with tonight. If he had any luck at all. The night and sleep over took Mikey Strongbow. Michael Conrad had died long ago.

He woke with a start and air sucking into his lungs. Fear overcame him and panic. He was wet with sweat and he could smell himself. He knew if he could smell this broken and bloody body so could everything else in the area. He tried to calm his breathing and gain control of his fear. Then he heard what had awakened him. The deep growling snort of a bear. He couldn't tell how close the bear might be, but even in the blackness of the night he understood the sniffing.

He had his back smashed up tight against the base of the shrub, the low branches covering him. He felt around the ground to either side of his body, trying desperately to find any kind of weapon. A stick or a rock. Gravel was all he found. Finally he felt a fist size rock near his right hand. He wrapped his fingers around the rock as tightly as he could. Holding his breath, he listened for the bear. "Where'd you go, you big devil? Come on; I'll give you some of this rock."

There was no sound, no sniffing, and no growling. Nothing but the sound of his own heart beat on his eardrums and the blackness of the night. Just as he let some air out of his lungs, massive jaws clamped down on his sprained ankle. Then there was nothing but screams. The rock in his hand fell short of the bear's snout. The broken leg was useless for any kind of defense.

It only took a couple of pulls from the Grizzly bear to pull him out from under the shrub. He was being dragged down the rock slide, the broken leg dragging along at an odd angle. Blackness swallowed Mikey into an abyss of unconsciousness.

The warmth from the sun woke him first. Then the choking coming from his own mouth and lungs as he spit dirt up. He reached up to find most of his upper body covered with a thin layer of dirt and pine needles. "Damn it! The bastard tried to bury me!"

He tried to sit up, but the pain was too much in his weakened state. "If only I had some water," was his thought as he laid his head back down. Then he heard the lumbering paw falls of the bear returning. "I shouldn't have moved. I know better."

It was too late. He opened his eyes to see the huge bear standing on his hind legs above him. He wanted to shut his eyes and make the bear disappear. Instead, the bear returned to all fours with a front paw on either side of his head. Mikey lost all control and peed himself as the bear opened his mouth. The smell coming from the bear reminded him of a woman's body when he had waited for three days before he found a good place to bury her.

The last thing Mikey Strongbow heard was the crunching of his own skull in the bear's mouth.

33

Augusta, Montana

The drive to Augusta was uneventful. They had traveled about ten or so miles on the interstate then exited off onto a state highway. A two lane road through wide spots made up small towns or communities, ranches, and plenty of wheat fields. As the sun came up completely, the views of the morning sun shining on the front range of the Rocky Mountains was breathtaking. John couldn't enjoy the views with the horrible fear that was building for the safety of his wife. Finally, the SUV in front of him slowed for a stop sign before making a rolling stop into a left turn. Another mile and they were entering Augusta.

Like most small Montana towns that survived on hunting season and the annual summer rodeo, there wasn't much to the place. A couple of stores, one gas station, a small old hotel, two bars, and the rodeo grounds. Most all of the other buildings were long out of business. Places with ghosts of better days peering through the dusty windows.

Wilson had pulled into a parking lot in front of a log cabin that had been remodeled and now housed a bar and restaurant. The lot was almost full of other SUVs and pickup trucks. There were even some four wheelers or ATVs as some folks called them. There was no shortage of emergency vehicles and sheriff cars. People were taking this very seriously. John didn't know if it was the concern for

Dawn or fear of such a story ruining their tourist and hunting season incomes. At this point, he didn't care; he just wanted to find Dawn.

One of the sheriffs had laid out a big map on the tailgate of his truck. Several men and women had gathered around the sheriff and map. Another sheriff was shaking Wilson's hand and commented on how long it had been since they had seen each other. "Duke Benhart, this is John," but before Wilson could finish, John took his hand and shook it.

"I'd like to take a look at the house."

"House?" Duke looked confused.

"The house where the stranger is caretaker for the elderly woman. Seems out of place if you are hired to look after a place that you would be standoffish with your neighbors. That sounds like someone that wants to keep to themselves." John took a cup of coffee that was offered to him.

"Keeping to your self isn't against the law, mister. Not in Montana, anyway." Duke smirked.

"I would be willing to bet in this small town there's not too many people that stick to themselves. More like everyone here knows everyone and their business, too."

Wilson smiled. "John has a good point, Duke. Let's go take a look at the place."

"We don't have a search warrant, Wilson. But since there might be a missing person involved, I think we can get away with looking without a warrant."

Duke talked to several other deputies and rescue people on a meeting place up near Sun River Canyon. Everyone would meet there in an hour. Duke, Wilson, and John loaded up in their respective vehicles with Duke leading the way to Old Miss Becky's house.

The three men parked bumper to bumper along the street in front of the old clapboard house. None of the homes in Augusta were new. In fact, many were well over a hundred years old. Miss Becky's house was no different. It sat on the north side of town, which was only about five blocks from Main Street that cut through the middle. The closest neighbor was almost two blocks away and there was nothing but a large wheat field behind her place. What was left of an old shed type building still stood behind the house on the edge of the field. It had seen better days, probably fifty years before.

Duke stepped up onto the wooden porch and knocked on the door. They all waited for any kind of noise from the inside, but there was nothing. Cupping his hands around his eyes and pushing against the glass in the door, Duke was hoping to see something, anything.

"I don't see any signs of anything." He reached down and tried the brass door knob and the door opened. "Well, just like most Montanans, he didn't bother to lock the door. Guess we should have a look around."

The little house was clean and neat. It didn't look like anything was out of place, not even in the kitchen. Someone had been cooking as the dishes had been washed and left to dry next to the sink. It looked like at least two people had been eating.

227

Wilson pulled the small refrigerator door open to seen almost empty shelves. John was looking inside the cupboards, which were almost bare, too.

They looked into the bathroom and the one bedroom and again found not much of anything. "Do you all notice anything strange?" John asked.

"Nope, not really." Wilson was scratching his head.

"If you are taking care of someone's house, wouldn't there still be some belongings of the owners in the house? Look around; there is no sign that an elderly woman ever lived here. Not one knickknack or photo."

"Maybe she took it all to Helena with her?" Duke said as he stepped out onto the back porch. "Hey, look here! A pair of woman's sandals."

Both Wilson and John tried to get through the backdoor at the same time, with John winning out. He looked at the sandals in Duke's hands while panic ran down his spine. "Oh my God! Those are Dawn's!"

Wilson looked at John. "Hold on, don't panic. You and Dawn have been apart for a good while. What makes you so sure those are hers?"

"Because I was with her when she bought them! They were her favorite pair; wore them everywhere because they were so comfortable. She always traveled in them, that's how I know!"

The three men searched the house in more detail, looking for any other sign that Dawn had been in the house or when she had been in the house. They came up with nothing.

Wilson was standing on the back porch talking on his cell phone, while Duke was calling deputies on his radio. John was pacing in a circle in the shade of the tall cottonwood trees in the back yard. "Damn it!" he cursed as he threw his baseball cap across the yard. It landed just a little ways from the broken down shed.

He walked over, stooped down to pick up the cap when he noticed the shed sported a new lock on the flimsy door. "Why would someone put a new lock on this old broken down shed?"

Instead of waiting for an answer from either of the other two men, he walked over and kicked the door. The rusted hinges broke loose and the door flew inward. As the dust cleared, he could see stacks of boxes, a few old trunks, and stacks of old clothes and suitcases. Then the smell hit him, almost knocking him over. Something in the old shed was dead.

"Please God, don't let it be her," John prayed. Wilson and Duke smelled the stench the same time they arrived at John's side. They both stepped backward.

Duke keyed his mic. "Boyd, get the ambulance over here at Becky's place and call the coroner, too. We're going to need both. Hold the guys out at Sun Canyon until further notice."

"10-4, Duke."

John had already started making his way into the shed. There was no rhyme or reason to the stacks of clothes. Some of the items looked new or never worn, while others looked like they belonged to Miss Becky when she had been a young woman. There were stacks of shoes both new and old. The closer to the trunks he got, the stronger the smell became. Then there was the buzzing. "Flies! Crap, there must be millions of them."

Wilson walked up to John's side. "We need to open these trunks, John, but I want you to let me do it, okay?" He didn't wait for John's answer. Instead, he reached for the first trunk. He opened the lid slowly. Relief came over both men when they saw more clothes and some keepsakes that looked thirty or forty years old. "I bet those belong to Miss Becky," Wilson surmised.

Duke had stepped over to the third trunk and opened the lid. Millions of big green flies flew out and into Duke's face. "Jesus!" He wanted to swat at them, but elected to hold onto the trunk's lid. There in the bottom of the trunk was a small body wrapped in a quilt.

Wilson grabbed the trunk's lid just as Duke lost the contents of his breakfast. The younger man ran for the shed's door, vomiting the whole way. John finally found the nerve to look into the trunk.

"Thank goodness. That's way too short to be Dawn's body and it looks like it's been in the trunk for a good while."

"I'd take odds that's Miss Becky. We need to contact her family in Helena to see if she's there with them or they think she's here. Time we step out of here and leave the scene for the state, boys.

I'll make some calls." Wilson was already digging his cell phone from his pocket.

Duke was leaning onto a cottonwood tree, trying not to vomit anymore. "Sorry guys; that was more than my stomach would allow. I never...."

"Don't be worrying about that. We need to worry about my wife and where she might be." John refused to think she was dead.

34

Montana

I woke as the sun was coming up. I was relieved to know I had lived through the night and Jake was still sleeping near my feet. I wasn't so happy that my shoulder hurt even worse than it had the night before. Jake felt me stirring and he, too, stood and stretched. I pulled my filthy shirt and jacket from my shoulder and looked at my bite wound. I still could not see the bite very well, but the redness had grown even larger. More serious, my arm and neck were swollen and there were large red streaks running down my arm. "Oh crap, Jake! It's not only infected, it looks like I have a good start on blood poisoning. Great, just great!" Jake cocked his head, looking at me like he might understand.

"Jake, we are going to go until we can't go any further. Since I'm all infected, maybe a bear will turn their nose up at me. You might, however, look like a nice snack. Keep an eye out, buddy. How about some berries and water before we go?"

I tried to fold the sleeping bag and tent one handed. Packing them away into the backpack was even harder. I pulled out some berries and some water. Both tasted wonderful, but the berries didn't stay with me very long. Before I could finish, my gut let me know it wasn't happy. Now I was suffering from a bad case of diarrhea. Was this the berries, something in the water, or the infection? Jake seemed alright. I guess it didn't matter what was causing my problem, surviving was the real task at hand.

I tried to slide into the straps of the backpack as easily as I could. All was good until the strap hit the infected area. I dropped the pack and went to my knees. "Guess I'll carry this like a sling on my good arm, huh, Jake? Let's get going."

We weren't making very good time. I knew I was burning up with fever, my arm ached, my neck was getting sore, and it burned with pain. I reeked to high heaven and my whole body hurt. The only thing to do, I kept telling myself, was to keep drinking and keep walking. Jake must have known the situation I was in as he never ran off. He would stop when I stopped. He was even a gentleman, turning his head when I had to suddenly drop my jeans. When I had to stop and rest, he would stop and sit beside me.

I lost count on how many times I had to stop and drop my jeans, but I knew the sun was getting lower in the sky. I did realize it had been a good while since the last stop, so maybe whatever was causing my problem was going away. I stopped to refill one of the water bottles. Looking at Jake, I explained, "The good news is that the creek is getting wider. The bad news is it looks like another night out here."

I found a good wide spot next to the creek to camp the night. I knew I wouldn't attempt to erect the tent—my arm and shoulder were far too painful to move much at all. Everything I did, I was trying to do one handed as not to move that arm. I was afraid to look at it again, but I looked anyway. There were three red streaks sticking out from the sleeve of my shirt. Soon they would be down to my elbow. "No telling how far up my neck the streaks are going."

I sat down on the pack with my feet stretched out. Jake by my side, I petted him with my good hand. Tears started rolling down my cheeks. I couldn't control the desperation any longer. Deep inside, I knew crying wasn't going to help yet the tears kept flowing. I was, in fact, sobbing. Jake started licking my tears away, but he couldn't keep up. "I'm a mess," I stuttered as tears and snot ran down onto my shirt, adding to the dirt and other smelly bodily fluids.

I took my t-shirt off, dipped it into the water, and placed the cool, wet cloth on my shoulder. I started to cry even harder. Holding the wet shirt there until the coolness left, I laid it on the top of a small bush to dry. I dug my jacket out of the pack along with the tent.

"Screw this, Jake. Tonight we get a fire. If he finds me, so be it. I'm freezing and need more heat than just you. Let's make a fire!"

It didn't take me too long before I had found enough fire building material to get the job done. After I had a small fire going, Jake and I gathered larger sticks and stacked them near the fire. By the time we had gathered enough dead branches to last most of the night, I was sweating like I had run a marathon. I finished off a bottle of water, relieved myself, and crawled into my nest of folded tent and sleeping bag. Again Jake curled up on the foot of the bag. He was sleeping in a matter of seconds. I, however, watched the flames dance just feet from my face. I knew I was running a fever, but the heat from the flames felt good on my freezing body.

Instead of falling asleep, fearing what might await me in the darkness, I let myself remember the many camping trips John and I had enjoyed. The many nights beside a stream with a nice fire and some good wine. How we would snuggle beneath a light weight sleeping bag in the Alabama summer night. How John would gently kiss me and make gentle, sweet love to me. "John, I never wanted anyone but you."

***I didn't know Susan and Robert Gilbert and I certainly didn't know they were camping up on the Gibson Reservoir. Susan and Robert had camped near the mouth of the creek as it dumped into the reservoir. Not many people would hike that far up the reservoir so it was always a nice get away for the two of them. Away from their jobs and the city. They had always thought about buying a cabin up in the area, but instead always found a great camping place on their week of summer vacation.

"Honey, look up there toward the mountain," Susan told Robert.

"Which mountain?" He snickered.

"There," she said as she pointed toward the west. "Where the creek comes down out of the mountains."

"Looks like a campfire. Guess we have company this year."

"At least they didn't get this spot. They're far enough away that they won't be able to hear our wild mountain sex tonight!"

235

"You're so funny. We're way too old for wild mountain sex on the ground, woman." They both were laughing and soon forgot about the small flickering fire not so far away.

35

Augusta

John and Wilson backed out of the shed as not to disturb the crime scene any more than they already had. Duke was still feeling green as the three men made their way to the front yard and their vehicles.

Wilson called for several deputies to come and stay at the house until the Coroner and investigators arrived to process the place. He also called for Bobby Gunter. He was the local Fish, Game, and Wildlife officer for the Sun River Canyon. Bobby arrived in a cloud of dust on the gravel road thirty minutes later.

After introductions, Wilson gave Gunter the run down on everything they had found. Wilson looked at Gunter and asked, "Where you think this guy might be holding up?"

"Geez guys, this will be like finding that needle in a haystack crap. I suggest we split into two teams. One checking on cabins on this side of the ranger's station and the other on the Benchmark side. There are more cabins on the Benchmark side, but more camping places on this side and near the reservoir. I know the locations of most of the cabins and who owns them, but that doesn't necessarily mean someone manic hasn't taken one over."

John was pacing again as he knew they were running out of daylight again. "We're running out of time, guys!"

"It's better to make solid plans and start tomorrow morning than to run off into the dark willy nilly," Wilson stated.

"I know, but…. but the longer Dawn is out there, the less chance we are going to find her alive."

"So, let's get a plan going," Gunter said as he reached for his radio. He called several rangers and made plans for everyone to meet at the River Lodge in an hour.

Wilson and Duke contacted the people already out near the lodge and gave them an estimated arrival time. The four men left for the lodge as soon as the replacement deputies arrived.

John was at the end of the parade of official vehicles, racing down the gravel road toward the lodge. He dropped back just a bit, tired of eating all the dust. Anyone within ten miles would be able to see the dust cloud they were making. He couldn't help but notice the beauty of the land. He topped a small hill to a breathtaking scene. Before lie a long gravel road and beyond that standing tall and mighty was the front range of the Rocky Mountains. The road was lined with what was left of Black Eyed Susans as he had always called the weed. The mountains looked almost blue. He now realized just how Dawn could have been taken in by a stranger with a promise of this view and a mountain adventure. Anyone would want to experience this place. "It should have been us, not you and someone else," he whispered.

In a trance from the mountains standing before him, he almost missed the turn off. He snapped to just in time to see the River Lodge sign with the arrow pointing to the road on the right. The dust cloud was now a good half mile ahead of him after the turn. He hit his breaks hard, whipped the SUV hard, and fish tailed into the turn. It was only his police tactical driving training that saved him from sliding off the gravel road. It wouldn't have hurt anything but his pride, as there were no ditches on either side of the road. Just a little deeper ridge of gravel and wide open fields. There wasn't even a fence to plow through. Straightening the vehicle out, he pushed hard to catch up with the others. He was soon eating their dust again.

A few miles down the road John could see a few cabins off a ways on both sides of the road. Some were boarded up, but those that were not showed no signs of life. They passed huge ranches, multi-million dollar spreads. The guest houses and bunk houses were larger than anything Dawn and he had ever lived in. "Probably some corporate get-a-way lodge. That one has a chopper pad," he was talking to himself again.

The parade had slowed as they approached a hair pin turn with a small damn on the right. Water flowing over the dam was running back toward the ranch they had just passed. On the upside of the dam he could see a lake forming. It wasn't long before he saw a campground on the small lake then a sign reading Sun River Lodge. Everyone was turning left.

As John made his left turn, his heart felt a renewal of hope. There were at least fifty vehicles, official and private, including a helicopter parked out in a field. By the looks of the crowd that was

239

gathered around, there were well over a hundred people, all dressed for a hard hike. He also saw several tracking dogs. The problem he saw was the sun was sinking below the mountains to the west. Darkness was closing in on the canyon.

There were several camping trailers, utility trailers, and even tents set up. There were two large open tents with tables and a portable kitchen set up. People started following Wilson and Gunter as they walked toward the open tents. Both men were being greeted and some handshakes were shared. Wilson jumped up on the tailgate of a pickup truck and pulled Gunter up to share the stage with him.

"Thanks for coming out this evening," Wilson began.

Someone from the crowd shouted, "More will be here in about two hours."

"That's a good thing, because we have a lot of country to cover and as you all know this is not going to be a walk in the park. We are not sure what we are dealing with or even where to look. What I can tell you is Miss Becky Roberts in Augusta was found dead a few hours ago. It wasn't a pretty sight as she had been dead for a while. We don't know if our missing woman is alone or with the man that may have killed Roberts. There is someone bringing some fliers with a photo of our missing woman. This is her husband John, here from Virginia."

John raised his hand and looked around. He tried not to make eye contact with anyone in fear he would see hopelessness in their eyes.

"Gunter has come up with a search plan. Gunter?" Wilson stepped aside and let Gunter take over.

"It's too late now to start any kind of search, so we will start at zero 430. I want two teams. Split up the rangers, police, dogs, and civilians as even as you can get on both teams. I want one team to start over by Double Falls and work their way up to the landing strip past Wood Lake. Lots of cabins back in there to search. Everyone will mark each door with a green ribbon so others know it's been cleared. The other team will start down by the Sun Ranch and work their way back here and then onto all the cabins and campgrounds up to the top end of the reservoir. Most places here have no cell phone coverage, but each team leader will have a radio and a satellite phone to keep in contact with either myself or Wilson. Now, I suggest everyone get some rest; it's going to be a long day tomorrow."

"I'll have breakfast ready at zero 400, boss," shouted one of the search and rescue women.

As the crowd started to disburse, John felt alone and empty. Helpless. He stood there not noticing Wilson standing beside him. "Come on, John; let's get something to eat and then some sleep. We're going to need it. You can stay with me. The Lodge gave some of us cabins until this is over. Nothing fancy. Just a cabin with beds and an outhouse. They are better than sleeping in the back of a truck and peeing behind a tree."

After a dinner of a MRE (meal ready to eat) supplied by the local rescue team, the three men sat in the small cabin drinking the two fingers of scotch

Gunter had poured into three coffee mugs. "This will help us sleep. It's been a hard, long day."

They didn't talk long, as all three were avoiding what was really on their minds. The thoughts of John's wife at the bottom of a ravine, or worse yet still dealing with the person that had killed Miss Becky and who knows how many others.

John emptied his cup and stood. "I think I'm going to turn in. I'm exhausted." Minutes later, he heard the other two men say goodnight and hit their bunks.

John was indeed exhausted with the events of the past two days. The sight in the shed was enough to cause nightmares for the most veteran officers and the thought that the most precious person in his life was somewhere with the person that caused the carnage was overwhelming. He fought the tears even though he was sure Wilson and Gunter would understand if they heard him crying. Sleep spared him the tears, but not the visions of Dawn calling for help as he tossed and turned long into the night.

"John, someone's at the door. Go answer the door, please," came Dawn's sweet voice. John could hear the banging. With a jerk, he was awake. The banging was coming from the cabin door. Hard, panic banging on the wooden door. Dawn's voice had just been a dream.

"Wilson! Wilson!" someone was screaming as they pounded even harder on the cabin door.

"What? I'm coming; hold on to your pants!" Wilson yelled back. John heard a chair turn over and Wilson, cursing loudly. "Damn it!"

By the time Wilson got to the door, Gunter had turned on the lights and picked up the chair Wilson had turned over. Gunter and John were standing in the middle of the small room in their boxer shorts looking at Wilson in his underwear, holding his duty pistol as he answered the door. "What?"

A young officer stood in the dark doorway looking relieved that he had finally woke the men up.

"Boss, you have to come and look at what we found. This is just plain wrong. Creepy wrong."

"What the fuck are you talking about, Dave? What time is it?"

"I don't know, three maybe. I think it was just after two when I left Augusta. It's a mess there. A big freaking mess, boss!"

"Let me put some pants on." Wilson turned to see that both John and Gunter were already dressed and sliding into their boots. It only took a couple of minutes for Wilson to return fully dressed.

"Now, you want to tell me what's going on?" The four men walked out of the cabin to see that half the camp was already awake from the truck flying into the parking area with full emergency lights flashing and the pounding on the cabin door.

"After the Coroner examined the body and it was taken away, the state boys started taking the place apart. Half the town was camped around the crime scene tape, waiting for any kind of news. They looked in every nook and cranny. They found more suitcases in the shed with different sized ladies clothes. They found some men's things in the back room of the house, tucked away nice and neat."

"So what is it you want me to see?" Wilson was trying not to sound irritated.

As they approached the back of a black and white SUV, Dave reached and opened the door. In a large plastic evidence bag was a six foot by four foot piece of plywood. There was something none of the men could make out stuck on the board. Dave reached in and pulled the board halfway out.

Gunter took his flashlight and shined the beam of light onto the plastic covering. "What the hell?"

"It's pony tails, sir! Freaking pony tails! The investigators said they were human hair pony tails! Told me to load them up and bring them out here to you. Wanted to know if the husband recognized one of them to be the missing woman's."

Wilson carefully pulled the plastic covering away from the board and started counting. There was fifteen various colors and lengths of hair all neatly displayed with pink ribbons holding the hair together. "Look, John, but don't touch, okay?"

"Gotcha," he confirmed as he took the flashlight from Gunter and started looking at each pony tail.

244

"I don't know. Hard to tell. I don't think so, but Dawn was always coloring her hair. The last time I saw her it was streaked, I think. Jesus, I just don't know." John could feel the color draining from his face.

"Okay. Boss, I need to get this back to the state guys. Everyone is talking DNA. They just wanted him to take a look. Oh, they found some empty beer bottles and wine bottles in the trash. They were still looking for personal stuff in the house when I left. Maybe they'll find something. See ya." The young officer pushed the door on the vehicle closed and headed to the driver's door.

John stood there staring at the tail lights as the SUV pulled out of the parking area. He could hear the whispers of the people standing around, no doubt whispering about the pony tails.

"It's zero 330, men. We might as well saddle up," Gunter announced.

36

Montana

I didn't realize I had fallen asleep until I jerked awake. I was burning up with fever, my clothes were soaked with sweat, I was shivering, and I felt sick to my stomach. Jake was still snuggled into the bends of my knees and I felt a little safer with him so close. His big brown eyes were looking at me, knowing I was awake and not well.

I only had a few larger pieces of broken branches to add to what was left of the fire. I peeled back the tent and sleeping bag and slowly stood. The night air hit my damp clothes sending cold vibrations through my entire body. I bent down to pick up the limbs, which made me dizzy. I knew the poison in my veins was spreading too fast for me to last much longer. Trying not to think about that, I placed the last of the limbs on the fire. As the fire grew, I stood close trying to warm my sick body.

I drank half of the water I had left out. It wasn't very cold, but it was wet and it felt good going down my parched throat. I poured a bit into my cupped hand so Jake could have a bit. He looked thankful then plopped back down on the bed we had shared.

"You think I need to lie back down, huh?" I asked, Jake's tail making a patting sound on the tent.

I set the bottle down and struggled to get back into the sleeping bag. Jake didn't want to move from his spot, but finally moved over enough for me to get somewhat comfortable. If only I had stood and faced the opposite direction of the fire. One 180 degree turn and I would have seen the campfire of the Gilbert's. I would have had hope. Hope that might have lifted my spirits. Hope that I might live through this after all

Instead, I closed my eyes to the dark, hopeless pit I had allowed myself to finally fall into.

"Jake, you will have to leave me soon and find your way back. I'm sure someone will find you and give you a good home. You are a great dog. A good friend. If things were different, I would take you home. But it looks like you're the only one that's going to make it ...."

37

Benchmark

The camp was alive with activity in the still darkness of the morning. John knew he had to eat and hydrate himself, but his stomach was sick with fear. All he could do was push the memory of the board with the ponytails attached as far out of his mind as possible. He managed to eat a bit of breakfast prepared by the rescue people. He was pouring his second cup of coffee when Wilson walked up.

"John, I would like you to go with us this morning. We just divided up the teams and our team will be taking the far side of the area. We have a bit of a drive over to where the cabins start, over by the Double Falls area and there are several camping places on the way we need to check out."

"Sounds good. I'm ready whenever you are," John tried to sound hopeful but his hope was fading fast.

"You can leave your rental here and ride with me." The two men, both with tall cups of strong coffee, headed for Wilson's SUV.

As John opened the door and the overhead light came on, he noticed the back seat was full. There were rescue supplies, including medical items, duffle bags full of who knew what, gun cases, rifles in the rifle racks, and shotguns in their place. Wilson had traded in his 9MM duty gun for a 44 magnum pistol. Before John could slide into the passenger seat, Wilson handed him a gun belt that held a 45 cal. Smith and Wesson.

"Thanks," John said as he buckled the rig into place. The cop in him took over instantly. He took the handgun, pulled the slide back, and a round popped into the chamber. He felt more at ease now that he was armed. He tried to push the thoughts of placing a 45 round in the middle of Michael Conrad's forehead out of his mind for now. They had to find Dawn first.

The two men loaded up into the SUV and lead their group of searchers toward the other side of the of the ranger's station road. They passed the turn off to the reservoir soon running out of what little pavement there was in the area. Wilson made several turns onto smaller gravel roads. John could feel the vehicle climbing, but had no idea what the elevation was or how much more they would climb. The headlights shown on several deer alongside the road as they made their way. What seemed forever in the mountain darkness, the parade of vehicles started making their way on a downward slope. Wilson finally pulled over into a field and parked.

As the group of searchers gathered around Wilson and John, daylight was seeping into the sky. John noticed it was cold up here even though it was late summer, but still above freezing by a good measure.

"I want everyone armed and ready to defend themselves. We have no idea what we are facing here, man or beast. We have one body already back in town and we are in bear country. I don't need to remind you of that. I want you four men to start down at the far end of the camp ground and work your way back here. John and you (pointing at a middle aged searcher that Wilson couldn't recall his name) come with me. We will start on the cabins. Everyone have their walkie-talkie? If you see anything, and I mean anything, that doesn't look like it belongs here, is out of place, or talk to anyone that has seen anything fishy, call. When we finish here, we will head over to the next campground. Any questions?"

Everyone shook their heads and started in their different directions. John noticed a couple of lanterns being lit and some flashlights popping on in the campground.

The first two cabins were locked up good and tight with no signs that anyone had been there for quite some time. By the time they made their way to the third cabin, they could see a pickup truck near the front. Wilson sent John around to the back of the cabin and kept the other man with him. By this time in the search Wilson was comfortable with John's police background and his performance.

Wilson stepped up on the front porch, trying not to make any noise, but the boards still creaked under his weight. He stepped to the side of the door and knocked. "Police!"

They could hear voices in the cabin. Sounded like a male and female, then some scuffling around. A lantern came on and then footsteps making their way across the creaking floor boards. "Just a minute," came the man's voice.

The door finally opened with a man holding a lantern, standing in his underwear and looking confused. "Police? What's the problem? Fire?"

"Your name, sir?" Wilson was shining his flashlight past the man into the cabin.

"Rick. Rick Farley."

"Are you alone, Mr. Farley?" Wilson could see movement in the cabin.

"No, my wife is with me. What's going on?" he demanded.

"Sorry to disturb you, but could your wife step out here?"

The man turned to call his wife, but she was already walking up behind him, pulling a sweatshirt over her pajamas. "What's going on, Rick?"

"Are you alright, Mrs. Farley?"

"Yes. Why are you way out here? Aren't you city police?"

"We are searching for a missing woman."

"Oh no. Rich, ask these men to come in," the wife offered as she stepped back.

Wilson called for John, but there was no answer. He yelled again, and then saw the flashlight come around the corner of the cabin.

As Wilson explained the situation to the Farley's, John was casually looking around the primitive building. No running water other than a hand pump on the side of an old sink built into an old cupboard on the side of the room. The bed was in the corner in the back of the cabin. There was no electricity that he could tell, no TV, no radio and no fridge, just a cooler by the cupboard. There were a couple of old chairs and a beat up sofa. There was

251

an old free standing cupboard they had made into an open closet of sorts. Everything they needed for a little get-away in the woods.

Wilson checked the couple's identification and suggested they pack up and go home until all of this was over. The Farley's thanked him for the heads up and promised to keep their eyes open for anything or anyone strange, and if they did see anything they would get in touch with the authorities.

The three men continued their search of the remaining cabins, but like the first two, they were all locked up tight with no signs of any recent activity. No vehicle tracks and no foot prints. They headed back to the meeting place by the campgrounds.

"Anything?" Wilson asked as he walked up to the group of men.

"Nope; just a couple of campers and they haven't seen anyone around here. A few cars and trucks heading up toward Wood Lake, but that's about it."

"Okay, you men check the campground before you get to the lake and we will take that old logging road that goes up to those old cabins in the gulch."

"No one has been up in that area for a long time, Wilson," one of the men spoke up.

"That's the kind of place our guy just might have taken over. When you get done with the campground, come our way. You'll probably get done there before we reach the cabins. Give me a

yell on the walkie-talkie when you start our way."
Wilson was already reaching for the SUV door.

38

East Side

On the other side of the ranger's station, the searchers were having the same kind of luck. They had checked all the cabins near the Canyon ranch and worked their way to the first campground on the little lake. They had talked to several campers, some in tents and some in trailers. No one had seen anyone that looked like they were up to no good. Two of the campers knew one of the search and rescue guys and joined in the search. The group had moved up to the next group of cabins near the reservoir road.

Susan Gilbert woke to the smell of coffee brewing and the sound of her husband whistling. She climbed out of their tent and stretched. It was going to be a beautiful day, she surmised.

"Ah, Sleeping Beauty awakes!" Robert handed her a cup of hot coffee with a big smile. "So much for that wild mountain sex last night. You were out like a fighter with a glass jaw last night."

"I did fall asleep right off, didn't I? But I had some crazy dreams." Susan sipped her coffee as she looked off to the far end of the reservoir.

"Breakfast?" Robert asked, but was already frying some bacon on the little camp stove.

"Sounds good. Robert, how long have we been coming up here and camping? Ten years?"

"About that, why?"

"In all that time, I can never remember seeing any campfires up near the end of the reservoir. It's pretty remote and wild up there. No real places to camp. I saw a fire up there when I got up to pee earlier."

"True, but we haven't been up there in a while. Mostly we hike to the northeast and stay here and fish. Maybe someone found a place to make a new camping area. There are others besides us that want to get away from the crowds."

"Crowds? All five or six other campers down in the other two campgrounds?" Susan was laughing. "Still it sort of bothered me."

"If it makes you feel any better, we'll walk up that way after we eat, clean up, and secure camp."

"No hurry. Now where's my food!?"

Susan had no idea that not far away, I was trying to sit up as the sun came rushing over the east peaks. Jake was still at my side. As I raised what I could of my body upward, he started sniffing at my shoulder.

"I know, Jake, I stink! And I'm hungry. I'm thirsty, too." I managed to find the water bottle. It was half full. I didn't care; I drank it down. "Jake, you're still healthy; you go down to the creek and drink."

I looked at his wet paws and realized he had already been down to the water. The fire was all but gone. I was too tired to even try to gather any limbs or to get more water. All I wanted to do was lie back down, so that's what I did. I slowly drifted back to sleep. I was done.

39

West Side

Wilson turned onto the gravel road, which led to the first cabin. These were the older cabins in the area. Most had been there for over a hundred years. There had been more, some taken by rock sides, a few by avalanches and some by wildfires. All had been there long before the airfield had been built at the end of the road for firefighting planes to land. Some of the cabins had been handed down from generation to generation, most with ninety-nine year leases. Those that were still standing were used for hunting lodges, but a few folks would come up here in the summer to spend time in the forest within walking distance of the lake. It was a beautiful place.

The first cabin wasn't boarded up, but it was locked up. There were a few truck tracks up by the side of the cabin, maybe a week or so old. Even though Wilson didn't want to destroy anyone's property, with one hard kick the door flew open breaking the lock. The cabin looked much like the Farley's cabin only not as nice. It looked like there hadn't been a woman's touch in the place for a long time. Empty beer bottles were scattered here and there in the make shift kitchen. However, there was electricity on this side of the road. There was an old electric stove and what looked like a sixty year old refrigerator. Wilson hit the light switch, but nothing came on.

"Power must be off at the box outside. People turn off the power then they leave. They don't want a short to burn down the cabin and the forest around them. Doesn't look like anyone has been here doing something they shouldn't, except maybe drinking too much beer."

The three men started their hike up the road to the next cabin. Parts of the structure were missing. It looked like an old snag of a pine tree had fallen and caved in the back half of the place. They walked on.

The road was going up at a steep incline. They had hiked in about a mile when they came up on the third cabin. To John's surprise, this cabin was well kept, newer looking, and even had a new roof. The owners had cleared a nice yard out away from the cabin to help protect it from a forest fire. "That's kind of funny, a fence out here."

Wilson looked over at John and asked, "Why not? A nice place to tie up your horse. Lots of folks come up here and ride the old trails down at the end of the road."

John was shaking his head. "I never would have thought of that, but I can see where people would enjoy that kind of riding."

Wilson stepped up on the porch and tried the door. It opened. He automatically reached for his sidearm. Slowly, he opened the door. The other guy stepped to the side while John eased to the back of the cabin. There were no windows or doors at the back of the building. Before John returned to the front, he could hear Wilson inside.

"Wilson? Anything?" John was hoping.

"Nope; it looks like someone just forgot to lock up. Probably doesn't really matter other than for insurance purposes because anyone really wanting in would just bust the door down like we did back there."

They hiked about two hundred more yards when they came to a fork in the road. To the right were two walls of what once had been a cabin. They turned to the left to see another cabin that was a total wreck, too. "Like I said, all old, no one taking care of them for years and now they are gone by the way."

John was feeling defeated. "Are there any more cabins up here, or is this the end of the line?"

"These are all that's up this road. There are a couple of places down by the airstrip, then nothing but miles and miles of nothing."

The middle aged man that had been tagging along with not much to say all of a sudden spoke up. "Hey, come and look at this."

"What ya got, Hank? It's Hank, right?" Wilson asked, trying not to look at the desperate look on John's face.

"Yep, Hank. But look here—tracks. Someone has been driving up here a good bit it looks like."

Wilson and John joined Hank, all three men looking at the truck tire tracks in the dirt. Most the gravel had washed away from the old road bed.

"I was pretty sure this was the last cabin. Maybe someone has gone and built something up here further, but I thought without a lease the State said no more building. Let's take a look see," Wilson said, John taking the lead again as Hank trailed behind.

The three men followed the dirt road for another half a mile. The road was now nothing more than two ruts going up the side of the mountain. Now looking more like a wagon trail, the road turned and then there was nothing.

Wilson stopped and, looking around, said, "Okay. I'm not the world's best tracker, but I'm not the worse either. Where in the hell did the road go?" Wilson was feeling out of his element for the first time.

John was examining the rocks and the trees, looking for any sign that there was a trail or road leading in any direction.

Now ahead of them a few yards came Hank's voice, "Come here! Come!"

They looked up and saw Hank throwing branches, like he was clearing a path. "Holy Crap, would you look at this!?"

John and Wilson stopped short, looking at the gate Hank had uncovered. On the other side of the gate the road was improved somewhat. Hank had already climbed over the gate when John and Wilson jumped up and over. All three men stopped short when they saw the pickup truck at the same time. Twenty yards up the road in a clearing that looked much like a little parking area sat a dark green *Ford* pickup truck.

"Easy boys. Just in case someone is around, let's not spook anyone," Wilson whispered.

The three men spread out and slowly approached the truck. John could feel his heart in his throat and wondered if the others felt theirs. Wilson and John had their guns drawn and aimed at the truck.

"This is kind of creepy; a truck out here in the middle of nowhere. The hair on the back of my neck is standing up," Hank admitted.

Wilson approached the truck first. "Clear." He then reached for the handle and to every one's surprise the door opened. Wilson searched the driver's side while John opened the glove box and started rifling through a few pieces of paper.

"Get this! Truck is registered to Michael Conrad. The address is the house in Augusta. Maybe, we are onto something." John sounded hopeful.

Hank was walking around the truck in a small pattern of a circle that got larger with each complete 360 degree trip. "I found a path!" he shouted, but then within twenty seconds, he called out, "Here's another one."

There were three different paths leading away from the truck. Only one looked as if it had been traveled a bit more than the other two.

"Wilson? What do you think?" John asked as he looked at the better traveled path.

"I can call for help, but we would be wasting time if we waited on the other team to get here.

They haven't called, so I think we can safely assume they haven't found anything and are still searching. I say we hike up this trail a bit and see what we can find. I can call the state guys in to process the truck."

"So you think our guy is out here and on foot?" Hank was still looking around the truck.

"Either that or he hid the truck out here and has left in another vehicle. When we ran NCIC on Michael Conrad, we came up with nothing. I left before anyone got any info on vehicles on him, but who's to say? He might have a vehicle registered in a different state or under a different name."

John was more worried now than before. "I don't think a dead man can register a truck. The question is who registered this truck here in Montana? The date on this registration is this year. Maybe two Conrads, but I doubt that—more likely two different men." Wilson started up the path with John and Hank following. "Keep your eyes peeled, guys. If this is heading where we think it is, we might be on a manhunt of a killer."

John already knew that, but just didn't want to think about Dawn being in the hands of a psychopath that hangs trophy ponytails on a board for safe keeping. He didn't want to think of her in the hands of anyone else.

40

East Side

Susan and Robert finished their breakfast and cleaned up their campsite. Robert put all the food away in the container they kept in the back of their pickup truck. Susan was packing up some water and snacks into their small packs made for hiking. It was a perfect Montana afternoon to hike around the reservoir. There were several other couples that had arrived for a day of fishing down by the dam.

"See, I told ya; place is getting crowded." Robert laughed. They grabbed their packs and headed down the path that would lead them around the reservoir and toward the mouth of the stream.

They soon ran out of easy hiking as the path ended and they had to make their own way. At times they were not hiking, but actually climbing over huge boulders and fallen trees. They had stopped to rest on a downed tree and to take in the beauty of the area. They were about fifty feet above the lake shoreline and had almost a full view of the mirror like surface of the water.

"Well, even if we don't find anything up by the creek, this was worth the hike." Susan took a drink from her water bottle. "I know you would rather be fishing."

"Yeah, those two couples down by the dam are catching my fish today!"

Susan stowed her water bottle, slid back into her small pack, and started to stand. Robert stood first and held out his hand to help her up. As she stood, he pulled her to him and kissed her. "You forgot to tell your husband you love him today."

"No I didn't. I called him while you were cleaning up camp."

They laughed at their regular joke. "Liar, liar, pants on fire. You know there's no cell signal up here."

"Caught me!" Susan smiled and turned to keep walking. Robert smiled and followed his wife. Neither one saw the official vehicles pulling into the parking lot down by the dam.

***

Gunter walked down the rock covered shoreline, down to where the young couples were fishing while the other men of the search party took a lunch break.

"Hey, catching anything?" Gunter called out.

"A couple of small ones; threw them back," came the answer from one of the men. The couple figured they were about to be checked for their fishing licenses and started pulling out wallets and items from their gear bags.

"No need for that, folks. I just want to ask you all a few questions."

With surprised looks, they all stopped what they were doing. "How long have you all been here today?" Gunter was facing west and had to shade his eyes from the afternoon sun.

"Got here late this morning. Why?" questioned the shorter of the two men.

"We got a woman missing out here. We think she might be with a man from Augusta. Mind if I see your IDs?"

Gunter checked out the IDs of the two couples. One couple was married and the other couple was friends from Great Falls. Gunter talked a while longer just to see if anyone got nervous or started acting suspicious. After about ten minutes of chit chat, Gunter felt like everything was on the up and up. Everyone seemed happy to be out here fishing and having a good time with one another.

"We have a search and rescue camp set up at the lodge. If you see anyone, please get down there with the information as soon as you can." Gunter started to turn to go back to the vehicles, as his stomach was growling from hunger.

"Hey Officer? There is a couple camped up the lake a piece. See their tent?" The taller of the men turned and pointed up the side of the reservoir. "I saw a man and woman up there this morning when we got here, but we haven't seen them or any movement up there in a while."

Gunter squinted through the bright reflection coming off the water and could indeed see a tent in the distance. "Thanks, we'll take a look."

After the short walk back to the vehicles, Gunter was greeted with a bottle of water and a sandwich. Taking a drink of the water, then a bite of the sandwich, he motioned with the hand holding the bottle toward the tent. "Got some campers up there to check on, but that looks like that's about everyone up here."

The search party finished their lunch and cleaned up after themselves. Some of the men decided to fan out toward the trails that led up into the forest to the Northeast while Gunter and four men walked up to the small camp site.

They reached the camp site and to their dismay there was no one in sight. Gunter checked the truck. It was locked. One of the deputies radioed in and had the plate run for ID. Gunter checked the tent and it was empty, too. Another deputy checked the back of the truck. "Hey Gunter, there's food in a dry box and a cooler back here. I bet they are off on a hike."

"Anyone find anything that might tell us which direction they might have gone?"

"No, but there seems to be a man and a woman camping. There are two different size shirts hanging on this line over here," another searcher called out.

Gunter felt like he was in a real dilemma and wasn't sure just what to do. He felt like he really needed to wait and check out this man and woman, but not knowing what direction they might have left in and not knowing how long they were going to be gone, he felt like any time he spent waiting would be wasted. They needed to press on, widen the search. There was one more campground to be searched before they got to the Bob Marshall Wilderness trail heads, then it was no man's land.

A few seconds later, the deputy's radio squawked. "Gunter, the truck belongs to Robert Gilbert. You know, Robert Gilbert from Gilbert Construction in town."

"Well, we still need to talk to them." He pointed at four of the men. "You four stay here with me and the rest of you go up and check to see if anyone is camping at the other campground. If you don't find anything, we'll all meet back at the lodge."

The men shook their heads, said their good-byes, and split up. Leaving Gunter and his group looking around for any signs of which way the hikers had gone.

41

West Side

Wilson, John, and Hank made their way up the small trail, trying to not to make any noise. The wind coming down the mountain and blowing through the pines was helping cover up what little noise they were making. Not a good idea in bear country, but the two legged monster they were hunting might be more dangerous than any bear, after all even in Montana bears were not armed. All of a sudden, Wilson stopped dead in his tracks. John and Hank stopped short on his heels.

"What?" John whispered.

"Look through the trees, one o'clock." Wilson had zoomed in on something. "Looks like a cabin."

"Up this far?" Hank asked in amazement.

"Looks fairly new compared to the others down at the bottom," John whispered.

"John, go right, Hank and I will go left." Wilson motioned and the three men started making their way to the front of the cabin.

There was no sound or signs of life coming from within the structure. John cleared the open wood shed and continued to the front corner of the porch. Wilson and Hank stopping at the left side of the porch, peeking around the corner. All three men tried to look in the windows, but all the curtains and shades were shut. As quiet as he could, Wilson eased up onto the side of the porch, pasting his back against the front wall. John managed the same maneuver.

"Jesus, I wish we had a SWAT up here," Wilson was thinking in a whisper. He motioned for John to stay put. John gave him a nod. In one huge side step, Wilson was beside the front door. He reached over and tried the door knob. It turned easily in his large hand. As the door eased away from the strike plate on the jam, he pushed with his shoulder. He jumped back a step and then kicked the door the rest of the way into the cabin. Wilson ducked and broke left, keeping close to the floor, screaming, "POLICE!"

As his eyes adjusted, he realized John was entering the room in the same manner, only breaking right in a low squat. Both men had their guns drawn and were scanning the room. Nothing!

"Cover me!" John shouted. He stood, took several fast steps to the first door which was the bathroom. Kicking the door in then jumping to the side of the door jam. Again nothing but a bathroom.

They cleared the whole cabin in the same manner including the closets. Finally, Wilson called for Hank, "It's all clear. You can come in now."

John was in the bedroom looking at the room, wondering if Dawn had been there when he noticed something in the closet. It was women's clothes, but that wasn't what really caught his eye. On the floor of the closet was a nice Brighton leather overnight bag. Brown tooled leather with turquoise trim. Just like the one he had bought her several years ago for her birthday. She had wanted that so much, but refused to purchase something so expensive for herself. So he surprised her with it to her delight.

Afraid to check the bag to see if it was hers or just one like hers, John knew he had to man up and look. He picked up the bag with the barrel of his gun and took it into the main room. He set the bag on the kitchen bar and reached for a kitchen towel.

"You think that's Dawn's?" Wilson asked, but he could tell by the fear in John's eyes that was what he was thinking.

In true Dawn fashion, there was her address on the ID tag, no name, just address. John could feel the blood draining from his head, causing a sick feeling in the middle of his stomach. "It's Dawn's; there's her address."

Wilson looked around the room. "John, let's not think the worse here. Look at this place. Not a thing out of place. No sign of a struggle, no sign that anything has gone bad here."

"That doesn't mean anything and you know it! Now what? We have no idea in what direction we need to even start looking." John walked out onto the front porch and looked off toward the mountains. "Freaking wilderness in all directions! You or anyone else didn't even know this place was up here!"

"Well, we know where it is now. We need to get back to the camp, check in with the others, get something to eat, take a little rest, and get a big search party up here at first light with the tracking dogs." Wilson desperately tried to sound hopeful.

"First light? Another night out there could mean her death if she is still alive!" John was crying.

"We can't go stomping around out here in the dark, John. You know that. This country is too rough. Someone could fall into a ravine or get caught in a rock slide and that would be the end of them or us. That isn't going to help Dawn either. We have to think smart out here. No second chances when ya make even a small mistake. Let's take a better look around the cabin and inside again and see if we can come up with anything else that might help." Wilson turned back into the cabin.

"Hank, do a sweep of the outside and see what you can find."

Hank nodded and walked past John, giving him a slight pat on the shoulder.

The three men searched the cabin and the area surrounding the building finding nothing that would lead to the real identity of the owner or squatter, whatever the case may be. Other than a few ladies bathroom items and the clothes in the overnight bag, there was nothing that would link anyone but Dawn to this place in the middle of nowhere.

Wilson did find some dog food, a bowl, and a leash. "Well, it looks like there is a dog involved in this mystery."

"I did see some dog tracks here and there, but none of them were very fresh. There were also boot prints down all three paths, but again, none fresh." Hank was scratching his head and wishing for more clues.

After about an hour of convincing John they should leave, the three men walked down to their truck. "As soon as we get back, I'll have the state boys head up here to process the truck and the cabin. They can do that in the dark. We sure as hell can't search up here in the dark." Wilson motioned for the men to load up.

42

Montana

My brain was awake and I knew I should get up and do something. Try and walk some more, gather some sticks, get a drink of water, just do something, but I couldn't. I hurt all over, my clothes were wet with sweat, my head was pounding, and I was so thirsty. I was afraid to talk. I could hear Jake panting, so I allowed my eyes to open just a bit.

Jake was standing a few feet away from me, tail wagging and holding a large dead limb in his mouth. I started to laugh. "Jake, I couldn't throw a stick for you if I tried."

Just like he understood what I was saying, he laid the limb down and sat there looking at me like I was the dumb one. "What? What you want, boy?"

He jumped up and took off toward the stream bank. I was too weak and sick to rise up and try to follow him. In a few minutes, Jake returned with another large stick.

"Jake, I think you might be the smartest dog in the whole wide world. Drop it!" He dropped the second stick. "Go find another one, Jake. Good boy! Damn dog is gathering firewood for me."

With a renewed feeling of hope, I forced myself up to a sitting position and looked at the pile of ashes that had once been a fire. Not all was lost, as I still had a couple of matches and I still had a bit of bark for kindling.

I tried to push myself up to a crouch, but my arm was swollen and red all the way down to my hand. It was of no use. My useless, infected arm swung away from my body, sending shards of pain up through my neck. I knew the infection and probable blood poisoning was racing through my body. My time was getting limited, more than I wanted to admit.

I wasn't sure how long Jake and I played the stick game, but after what seemed like the whole day, we finally had a good size stack of wood. Not enough to get us through the night, but enough to maybe keep the critters away part of the night.

"God, I'm hungry. It's a good thing you are earning your keep or you might be dinner!" Again, just like he knew every word I had spoken, Jake came over and licked my cheeks. He knew I was just talking for the sake of talking.

I gathered enough strength to get a fire started. "I might be dying, but I can still build a mean fire, huh, Jake?"

Once the fire was burning well enough that I knew it would last for a while, I made my way back the few feet to the sleeping bag and tent nest. I propped myself up into a half sitting position just because my back was so sore from lying on the rocks for so long when something caught my eye. At first, I thought it was just my imagination, but then I saw it again. A reflection! A flicker of bright light, but then it was gone. I rubbed my eyes, trying to focus on where I thought I had seen the shining bit of light. How far away? Were my eyes playing tricks on me? Maybe it was just the sun shining on a leaf or a reflection off the water.

"There! Jake, did you see that?" Jake jumped up and was looking around our little camp site. He picked up a stick. "No Jake! I think it's a reflection." But I couldn't be sure.

"Maybe it's a hiker?" I knew I had to do something. I was too weak to cut or break any live branches from the bushes to make some smoke. "Jake! Bring me a stick."

He did just that, a dead stick just like the others. I needed a live, leafy branch. Instead, I rolled out of my sleeping bag, tent nest and pulled on the sleeping bag. "This will have to do! It will make smoke!"

I pulled myself and the sleeping bag over to the fire. I threw the end of the bag on half of the fire, which allowed the sticks to keep burning, but caught the bag on fire at the same time. If this didn't work, if no one saw the white smoke that was billowing above my head into the air, I wouldn't make it through the night with just the tent over me, not even with Jake sleeping next to me. This was my last ditch effort and I knew it.

What I didn't know was just a couple hundred feet away, Susan and Robert had finally made their way up to the mouth of the stream where it dumped into the reservoir.

Susan had her head down, following Robert as he broke trail along the stream's edge trying to find the easiest path to follow. Susan just happened to look up and saw the white smoke climbing skyward through the trees.

"Look!" Is that a campfire? That's a lot of smoke for a campfire. It wasn't there a bit ago. Maybe that's the fire we saw last night."

"Whatever it is, it's throwing off a lot of smoke. Come on, step it up a bit. If it's not on purpose, we need to put it out before it gets out of hand."

The couple hiked as fast as the terrain would allow. They were still climbing over fallen trees, huge rocks, and every size of dead fall and sticks one could imagine.

All of a sudden, Jake started barking. He scared me so that I jumped up. I almost fainted from the pain in my shoulder and arm, but I managed to keep my balance. I thought I heard people coming through the brush. I reached over, picked up the last of the sleeping bag, and slung it into the fire. More smoke started filing upward. Jake didn't leave my side, but kept barking.

From a distance I heard two voices, a man's and a woman's. "Hell-o! Anyone there? Hell-o?"

Before I would answer, Jake took off downstream, barking and wagging his tail. I had to rely on his intuition that the people breaking through the brush were here to help.

I was trying to call for help, but just a slight whisper escaped my dry throat.

"Look Robert! A black lab! Hey boy, come here!" Jake almost knocked Susan down with excitement.

"Whoa, fella." Robert tried to calm Jake down, but he wasn't having anything to do with that. Jake ran circles around the two strangers while he cried as if he was crying for joy.

Susan broke through the last of the small brush when she spotted the smoke, the fire, and last of all, a woman. "Hey! We saw your fire. You need some help?"

Before I could reply, I fell to my knees. I'm not sure which was worse, the pain from my knees landing on the rocks of the stream edge or the pain shooting through my body from the jar of my arm and shoulder. Whichever one it was, it caused me to slip into blackness.

Susan broke into a jog toward the crumpled body lying on the rocks. Jake took off in a full run, leaving Robert to bring up the rear.

As Susan reached the body, she shouted, "ROBERT! It's a woman! Oh my God! It's a woman!"

Susan knelt beside the almost lifeless body of a battered, bruised, bloody, and filthy woman. Before she spoke a single word, she checked to see if the woman was still breathing. She had to look very close to see the ever so slight movement of her chest. Jake was now sitting on the other side of the woman. Robert was now next to them.

"Is she alive?" Robert feared the worst.

"Yes, but she's in bad shape. Robert, run for help! I'll stay here! Run and make it fast!

No other words were needed. Robert dropped his small pack and took off as fast as the rocky terrain would allow. Susan watched as he disappeared into the brush, heading back down to the lake.

Susan took the bandana from her neck and dipped it into the cold stream water a few feet away. As she walked past the fire, she tossed some limbs on the still smoking fire. Kneeling and then sitting next to the woman, she propped the unconscious woman's head up on her lap.

"We're here now. You're going to be okay," she whispered as she patted the dirty, sweaty forehead of the woman. "We got ya."

43

East Side

Gunter and his men had scouted the area with no hint of the direction the couple had hiked. A feeling of despair was creeping into each of them, fearing something terrible had happened and no one would be found alive.

The men were taking a break, trying to figure out what to do next or how long to wait, when one of them jumped up. "Look!" he shouted, pointing toward the upper end of the lake.

They all looked. Gunter grabbed his binoculars and zoned in on the image. In the round frame of the glasses, he could see a man running in their direction. A few seconds later, the man must have seen them and started waving his arms as he ran.

"Grab your gear, guys! We might have something!"

Once Robert thought they were in hearing distance, he started shouting at the men jogging in his direction. He ignored the pain in his ribs and stepped up his run. "HELP! We need help!"

Gunter started shouting back. "What has happened?"

By the time Robert met the small group of men, he was totally out of breath and bent over, resting his hands on his knees, taking in great long breaths.

"Are you alright?" Gunter asked.

Robert held his hand up, with his index finger extended in the international sign for, 'just a minute.'

Finally, Robert found enough air to speak. "We found a woman. She's in bad shape. Like really bad shape. Doesn't look like bear, but she been through hell by the looks of her."

"Who's we?" Gunter asked.

"Sorry, my wife. Susan, my wife, stayed with her." Robert turned to look up toward the mouth of the stream. "She's gonna need Life-Flight, if she makes it."

"Is there room enough up there for landing?" Gunter asked, but he already knew the answer. They would have to carry the woman out of the brush and get her up to the parking area at the far end of the reservoir.

"No; it's pretty thick up there," Robert started walking toward the two women hidden by distance and brush.

Gunter was already on the radio, talking with base camp ordering Life-Flight into the air.

Gunter radioed Wilson first. The static made it almost impossible for the two men to talk. "Found woman near Reservoir," Gunter yelled.

"REPEAT!" Wilson could hear the desperation in his voice; then the radio went silent.

44

Reservoir

Wilson threw the microphone he was shouting into on the dash of the truck. He pressed the gas pedal to the floorboard. The truck was fishing tailing down the hill toward the cut off that lead up to the reservoir.

"He said reservoir, no?" Before John or Hank could answer, Wilson had turned, heading up to the lake. The road was now paved and he could drive a little faster than the gravel road had allowed, but the turns and curves still slowed them down.

As they topped the hill, they could see a few of the search and rescue people marking off a landing zone, which meant someone was being rescued by Life-Flight out of Great Falls. That could mean many things, but the most important thing was whomever they had found was still alive.

John was whispering, "Please let it be her. Please let it be her."

None of the men dared to say it could be anyone, or maybe even a bear attack or a hiker that had fallen. Secretly, everyone in the truck was praying it was Dawn.

John was out of the truck before Wilson could shove the shift lever into park. He jumped out of the truck, hitting the pavement at a full run toward the largest group of people.

"You all found a woman? A WOMAN?" John was looking in all directions.

Finally, one of the search and rescue people spoke, "Two campers taking a hike found a woman. Gunter and the others are up at the far end of the lake. They will have to carry her out."

"Anyone know who she is or what she looks like?" John was almost yelling.

"No, sorry. We just know it's a woman. We don't know what kind of injuries. We do know that Life-Flight is on the way in. It should be here shortly." The man turned back toward the other rescuers.

John started off toward the end of the lake. Gunter wanted to grab him and tell him no. Wait here, but he figured it would be of no use. Instead, he reasoned, "John, wait up."

John stopped, looking at Wilson with tears in his eyes. "What?"

"I know you want to run off and see for yourself. Can't blame you there. But the men up there are the best Montana has to offer. Not only are they search and rescue, but there are several paramedics on the team. They will need room to work. We need to wait here. Stay out of their way and let them do what they are the best at, saving lives." Wilson reached out for John's shoulder.

"I know. I know. I'm scared! What if it's not her? What if it is her? The not knowing is the worst!"

"Okay, how about we walk up toward the end of the lake? We can at least meet them half way."

The two men started walking. Neither saying a word, both praying it was Dawn and she was still alive.

45

Rescue

I thought I was dreaming again. I was almost sure of it. I had dreamed I saw two people and Jake and I could feel someone pressing something cold on my forehead. I tried to speak, but only parched noises came from my cracked lips. I tried to lick my lips, but there was no moisture to be found. My tongue felt like a dry piece of beef jerky.

Then I heard some water, or so I thought. Again, I must be dreaming.

"I got ya. I got ya. Here," came a soft voice.

At the same time I felt something cool and wet pressing against my lips. A few drops of water hit my beef jerky tongue. After a few drops, I managed to open my eyes. Well, one of them—the other one was matted over with who knew what?

"Ja… Ja… ake?" The word barely left my mouth when I felt Jake's nose on my cheek.

"Yes, you have a wonderful dog. He found us and brought us to you." The woman was smiling at me.

I tried to smile back. "Who…?"

"I'm Susan. My husband has gone for help. It shouldn't be long now. Try to rest."

"Da… Daw," was all I could force from my mouth. Rest was all I could do. I was fading fast. I knew just what terrible shape I was in and how horrible I must look and smell. I couldn't form another word.

"Big stick," came a voice from the blackness. I felt something stick me in the neck. "There, finally in! Sorry, I didn't have another choice on where to stick you," explained a man.

It was a struggle to open my eye. The images were blurred. I blinked a few times and was finally able to focus enough to see a woman and four or five men kneeling around me. Jake was near as I could hear his panting. I tried to reach for the pain in my neck, but my arm would not move.

"Don't try to move. Let us do our job," said one of the men.

"We need to get some antibiotics in the saline bottle. Looks like real bad sepsis and a few other things."

Susan looked at the young man and asked, "Sepsis?"

"It looks like she got a real bad bite and it has caused sepsis, ah, blood poisoning. We need to clean that area a bit before we move her. I don't think the chopper has arrived yet."

I tried to calm myself as they removed my clothes from the waist up, but the smell that was reeking from my body was making me sick. One man poured some liquid over my shoulder and arm and then patted the bitten area dry. I remembered someone applying some kind of bandage and then spreading a blanket over me.

The last thing I remembered was people trying to lift me up before everything went black.

46

Reservoir

The three men had made their way along the shoreline toward the mouth of the stream. No one said anything, in hopes of hearing the rescuers coming through the brush or the sound of the Life-Flight making its way into the canyon.

"John! Let's wait here!" Wilson finally broke the silence.

John stopped, turned to look back at the men he had depended on for the last few days. The men that had given him hope when all else seemed hopeless. All of the information he had learned, the dead woman in Augusta, Dawn's things found in the unknown cabin in the middle of nowhere; all of it leading to the thought that Dawn would be found dead. He had to make himself depend on them just a while longer. No matter how much he wanted to make a break for it and run for the area where the rescuers had gone, he needed to stay.

Just as he was about to turn and face away from Wilson and Hank, he saw the expression on their faces light up. He turned just in time to see two men, one Gunter, breaking through the brush twenty yards away. Behind them were two more men carrying a stretcher by the handles on the end and two more men bringing up the rear of the stretcher. There was a person on the stretcher. Not a body in a bag, but a person lying under a blanket.

John felt his chest tighten with fear. "Please God, please let it be her."

"WE FOUND HER!" yelled Gunter. "WE FOUND HER!"

John broke into a run with Wilson and Hank on his heels. He crossed the twenty yards in record time. Stopping just short of the stretcher, John could hardly believe what he saw. His stomach knotted up into his throat, almost causing him to vomit. The fear of not finding her alive became the fear of not being able to keep her alive.

He reached under the thin blanket and found her hand, holding just tight enough that she might be able to feel his touch.

"Dawn, Baby, it's me." No response from the woman on the stretcher. John had to look closely to make sure it was really her.

Her hair looked like it had been cut with sheep shearing scissors. Short tuffs of hair covered with blood, dirt, and pieces of pine needles. Her body was also covered in blood and dirt except her forehead where it appeared someone had wiped some of the dirt away. Her lips were cracked and sunburned. Her lower lip had split open and bled in a couple of places. There was an IV line in one side of her neck with a tube leading up to a bottle of fluids, held by one of the rescuers. The other side of her neck was red and swollen, with a bandage in the crook. The bandage looked fresh and new, leading down onto her shoulder.

"My God, what kind of hell have you been through?" John couldn't take his eyes off her, the woman he loved so much. "God, just keep her alive.

288

I'll give up any kind of second chance if you'll just keep her alive," he prayed, trying to make a deal.

John didn't realize that they had walked the distance from the mouth of the stream to the top of the parking lot. His only focus was on any sign of life from the broken body on the stretcher. There was only the rise and fall of her chest and the heat her fevered body was giving off.

He didn't hear the Life-Flight break the ridge top, coming in for a landing in the middle of the parking lot. It wasn't until the helicopter started kicking up sand and small rocks that John came out of his trance.

"Sir! Sir, you have to let go of her." It was one of the medics from the chopper. "We need to get her loaded up and to the hospital."

"Carlson!" Wilson yelled at the medic. "That's her husband; let him fly!"

The medic nodded his head at Wilson. "Sir, come on. You first!"

John looked up as they were almost to the door of the chopper. Finally letting go of her hand, he turned and jumped up into the door. The other two medics loaded the stretcher up onto the floor of the chopper, jumped inside, and slid the door closed.

One motioned toward John and the seat. "Strap in!"

John did as he was told as he watched the two medics start working, trying to stabilize their patient. No one except the pilot felt the chopper leave the ground.

47

Great Falls

The beeping sound was driving me crazy. For crying out loud, what was that horrible beeping keeping time with my very own heartbeat? Along with the unyielding beeping there was a hammer beating the inside of my skull. I could hear the faint voices of two men talking. One sounded like John.

"She isn't awake yet. The doctors don't seem to be too worried considering what her body has gone through."

I struggled to open my eyes. After a considerate effort, I finally opened them. Then with another effort, I focused both eyes. Looking around, I realized I was in the hospital and the beeping was a heart monitor hooked up to me. Well, that was a good sign. At least my heart was beating.

I tried to move a bit, but there were wires everywhere. I did manage a whisper, "John?"

Within seconds, John and another man were standing beside my bed.

"Nurse!" John and the other man yelled at the same time.

John took my hand in his and squeezed. "You're going to be alright."

As all of the horrible events started racing back into my mind, I could hear the beeping accelerate. "John? When did you…..?

"Honey, you need to rest."

The nurse walked in and ordered John and the other man to leave the room. I didn't want John to leave.

"No, John can stay."

"Wilson, I'll call you just as soon as she feels like talking and the doctors say it's okay." John sounded more like he was giving orders instead of requests.

"The sooner we can talk to her, the better, John. Call me." Wilson left the room.

"John, who was that?"

"Great Falls Police. He's the man that helped me find you. Him and about a hundred other wonderful people."

The nurse allowed John to stay in the room while she and the doctors examined me, finally giving me the okay to sit up as long as I could or wanted. After the nurses and doctors left the room, John walked over and sat on the edge of the bed. I could see the concern in his eyes.

"Guess I'm lucky to be here, huh?" I tried to smile.

"Very lucky. I'm not sure if you want to know everything." John took my unbandaged hand and held it tight.

"I'm not sure you want to know everything and I'm not sure if I want to remember it all. How about you call that police officer so I can just tell this once?"

Wilson came back, introductions were made, and he produced a recorder. "This is an official investigation and I'm going to record your statement."

I agreed.

"I'm going to turn on the recorder and ask you to state your whole name and date of birth. Then I'm going to ask you to relate all of the events leading up to you coming to Montana and everything that happened after you arrived."

I looked at John. "Everything?" I knew there were going to be a lot of painful parts that he probably didn't want to hear.

"Everything," Wilson instructed.

John looked at me the way he once looked at me, with all the love a man could have for a woman. "It's okay, Baby. Tell it all. We'll make it through together."

I started with the night Cindy and I had too much wine and she hooked me up on Mr. Perfect.com. How it had started out as a joke, something funny to do. Somewhere in the first few minutes, I had asked John if he had called Cindy and he assured me he had and that we would call her later in the evening.

I tried to remember everything Michael had told me about his life and the Internet inquiries I had made about him. The conversation and memories grew more uncomfortable as the story progressed. I held it together until I got to the part about my hair getting hacked off. I don't remember if they were tears of anger or fear coming back into me. I let go of John's hands and ran my fingers through my still dirty, nasty hair. I really needed a shower, even though it looked as if someone had tried to clean me up fairly well.

Wilson explained to me that once they got me to the hospital, the nurses took all sorts of samples from my body, including a rape kit and DNA samples from my fingernails and other areas of my body. Then after they treated my wounds, they finished cleaning me up as best as they could. After all, getting my hair washed and a shower wasn't going to happen with me unconscious.

Two and a half hours later, Wilson reached over and turned the recorder off. "Thank you for your statement, Dawn. If we ever find the SOB, this will put him away for a long time."

"Are there others?" I had a horrible feeling that I was the lucky one and there were others that didn't make it out alive. I could tell Wilson and John didn't want to answer me, but I had to know.

"Yes. The elderly woman whose house he had taken over in Augusta is dead. The search and rescue people from the county and the state are all up at the cabin looking for bodies and graves in the area."

"You think he might still be alive?"

"Could be he wasn't as bad off as you thought. I'm heading up there in the morning. Going to see if we can find the slide area you mentioned. I don't hold out much hope, too many rock slides in that area. Time will tell."

"Wilson? What if he's still alive?" I tried to control the fear in my voice.

"You just have to worry about getting well. I'm not leaving you alone." John leaned down and kissed me on my forehead.

"John, I'm out of here. I'll keep in touch. I'll see you before you leave." Wilson shook hands with John, nodded his head at me, and left.

"Honey, you really need to rest. I'm going to be right here in this chair; I won't leave."

"I need to go to the bathroom," I said, making an attempt to sit up straighter.

"No you don't. You have a catheter," John said sternly.

"What…?"

"You have a terrible case of sepsis. They are treating with antibiotics. When they took blood samples this morning, they said things were looking better. You needed several places stitched up, but since the wounds were several days old, the doctors said they would heal on their own. You might need to see a plastic surgeon later. You have a sprained ankle and a broken collar bone. More bruises than anyone could count. Your kidneys were not happy the first two days, but they seem to be working much better now."

"First two days? How long have I been out?" I wanted to cry, but I choked back the tears.

"It's been four days. Like the doctor said this morning, now that you are awake, things are really looking up. Right now you need to get some rest. It's been a long, stressful day and the doctor said no stress!"

John lowered my bed a bit and turned on the TV. He pulled the chair up closer to the bed so he could sit with his feet resting on the side of the bed like an ottoman. I don't remember much of anything after that, just a dreamless sleep.

48

Elk Season

Montana

November was looking like good weather for elk season this year. Cold weather and snow had already hit in the high elevations, driving the elk down to the lower fields. Joe had drawn a bull tag and was enthusiastic about him bringing some meat home.

Joe had a small leased piece of land not far from Wood Lake, where he had set up a little base came. He had packed a survival backpack the night before as one never leaves for the back country without one. Before it was even daylight enough for anyone else to make their way, Joe was up and gone.

It took him most of the morning to reach the top of the ridge that was scattered with small patches of snow. Town hadn't even seen the first flake, but up here was a different story. He was constantly eye on the sky for bad weather moving in while scouting for any signs of elk. It took him most of the morning to reach the top of the ridge. Still not seeing anything to shoot at, Joe decided to stop for lunch. He stopped at the edge of an old rock slide.

Sitting on the rock warmed by the late fall sun, he enjoyed the peace and solitude of the mountains. How anyone would want to live anywhere else other than Montana he just couldn't understand.

As he stood to stretch his legs, he noticed something reflecting in the sun just on the other side of the slide. "I wonder what that might be. No elk around; I might as well check it out," he said to himself.

Joe stowed his water bottle and sealed food pack into this backpack. Very carefully, he walked across the slide area, paying attention to every placement of each footstep. He didn't need to fall out here. No one would ever find him, even though he had left a note back at camp with the general location of his hunt today.

A few feet away from the shiny object, he realized what he was looking at. "Holy cow. That's a belt buckle."

He bent down and picked up the buckle and what was left of a man's leather belt. The belt had been chewed in two. There was dried blood on the leather. Joe held on to the belt and started looking around. A few feet away there was a long white rod lying beside a rock. "What the…?"

When he realized he was looking at a large human leg bone, he fought back the sick feeling in the pit of his stomach. A few yards down the slide, he could see what looked to be the remains of a man's body. Clothing that had once covered the man was now in shreds with most of the material missing. He could see a boot about ten yards away from the body, but no signs of the other boot.

The bones had been scattered and eaten clean for the most part. As Joe walked closer to the scattered mess, he lost his lunch as he almost stepped on what was left of a skull. He had stopped just in time as not to kick the skull and turned quickly enough so he didn't vomit on it. As he stood leaning over with his hands on his knees, hoping he was done throwing up, all he could think was, *Ah crap, there goes hunting for the rest of the weekend.*

As badly as Joe wanted to hunt today, he knew he had to make it back to Augusta to the game check station and report the body, or what was left of the body. Thank goodness it was near freezing and things didn't smell, or he would really be sick.

Joe made his way back up the slide and started hiking back to his base camp. He marked his way every few yards so who ever came back up here could find the body. Deep inside he was hoping no one would ask him to lead the way, but chances of that not happening were slim to none.

Making his way back down to his base camp was a faster hike than going up and he soon was in his truck, heading to the game check point. It looked like they might be able to get back up there before dark, maybe.

49

Virginia

I sat in my oak rocker, looking out over a valley that worked its way into the Shenandoah Valley west of Richmond. I had fallen in love with this view the very first time I had seen it. The old farm house had been ours for almost three weeks. It was June, hot but not very humid as of yet. I sat listening to John talking on the phone in the kitchen. I was wishing he would hurry the conversation and bring the coffee he had promised a bit ago.

His voice sounded far away like it did that day I woke up in the hospital nine months ago. So much had happened during those months it was hard to keep things in order. I had spent another four days in the Great Falls hospital before they would let me fly home to Virginia. I had to promise that I had someone there to take care of me because I had a long road ahead of me. John promised the doctors I would be in his care.

From the moment we left the hospital, he did everything in his power to make sure I was comfortable and in need of nothing. Two days after we got back to Richmond, he moved us into the guest house that belonged to his parents out at the lake.

I spent my days on the deck, drinking in the fresh air from the lake and the salt water from the bay only a few thousand yards to the south. It took longer to heal than expected. Dad was in remission with his cancer and he would sit with me on the deck for hours at a time. He allowed me to talk about the events in Montana when I wanted. I believe we were each other's therapists.

John never brought up the second chance with me and I never mentioned it again either. It all came so very natural. We did talk about all the things that caused us to part in the first place and vowed that those things would never happen again. Most couples never got a second chance. We almost didn't, so we hung onto every moment just in case it might be our last.

John found a job just before Thanksgiving in Richmond. We gave up the guest house for an apartment on the west side of town. The day after Thanksgiving we got a phone call from Wilson. My stomach knotted as he told us of the scattered human bones and bits of clothes a hunter had found on a rock slide. I remembered the shiny belt buckle that Michael had worn. I fought to keep the memory of him cursing me as I walked away, leaving him tangled and crooked at the bottom of the rock slide. Wilson told us they had sent all the remains off to the state labs for testing against the DNA they had collected from me.

Wilson had also explained that the search parties had found six shallow graves in and around a meadow not far from the cabin. The weather had turned to winter, but they managed to extract the bodies. The remains of those six graves had been sent to the state labs. Everyone just had to wait.

In May, Wilson had called, telling us that the searchers had started their hunt for more graves, as the weather had finally calmed down. It had been a long hard winter in Montana. Then he gave me the news that the state crime lab matched the DNA samples from me to the bones that had been found.

I couldn't talk anymore and handed the phone to John. I felt sick. I had been the cause of another human dying. My heart said he deserved to die a slow painful death. I had been lucky to escape, but so many others had died by his hands. I had to stop blaming myself for his death. He was going to kill me.

Now, here I sat in late June waiting for John to get off the phone. By the tone in his voice, I was sure it was Wilson on the other end.

"Here's your coffee." John handed me the cup as he sat down in the oak rocker next to mine.

"Wilson?"

"Yes. He got a phone call from a police department in Georgia of all places. Seems they have a young man in their jail accused of raping and killing some women. His DNA is almost a complete match from Michael's."

Fear jumped into my throat. "NO! He's dead!"

John grabbed my hand before I could run. "He is dead! Dawn, stop! He's dead."

"How can that be? The DNA, I mean." I took a drink of my coffee in hopes to settle myself down some.

"Wilson went into a long detail, but the best way I can explain is that they think the man in Georgia is this Michael's son. They learned his

302

father, who he never knew, was his mother's cousin. Jesus, how's that for a family tree?"

"Then they know who Michael really is?" I struggled to breathe.

"Yes. They believe his real name is, Michael Strongbow. The man in Georgia said according to his mother, his daddy's name was Mickey Strongbow. In either case, it looks like they got two killers off the street."

"Strongbow?" I heard myself whisper. "It was all a lie, but then I guess I knew that a long time ago."

"Honey, we can put all of this behind us now. He's dead, his son is going to be in jail a long time, and, well, we are going to be just fine." John stood and pulled me to my feet.

I knew what John was saying was true, but I still could not help but ask, "How many others, I wonder?"

"Wilson said he had received six more calls from other police departments once the DNA started running through the system. So there's no telling. But I really don't want to know. All I want is to put all of that behind us and concentrate on our life now."

As I stood on the back porch of our lovely home on the hill in Virginia, snuggling in the arms of the man I loved, I knew that was all I wanted also.

"You are absolutely right!" I pulled away so that I could look up into John's eyes. "Your folks,

Cindy, and Robert will be here soon. I better get busy in the kitchen."

"I'll shuck the corn so you can get the potato salad put together."

As we turned to the back door, John looked over his shoulder and whistled.

"I wonder where that dog went to this time. I hope he hasn't been in the creek again, so soon after we just got the last ear infection cleared up."

"Well, the vet in Montana said he was prone to ear infections since he was a pup."

We both broke into laughter as we saw Jake heading toward the house as fast as he could run, wet from nose to tail, ears flopping and his jaws doing the same thing, showing all his teeth. He looked like he was smiling and I suppose he was.

We all smiled a lot these days.

About the Author

K. D. Bloodworth grew up in a small town not far from Ann Arbor, Michigan, a city enduring a serial killer history. Since leaving her hometown, she has lived in seven different states across the country, finding adventure every place she called home. Her love and knowledge of the outdoors gave K. D. the insight for MrPerfect.com. K.D. has been able to reach into her memory of survival skills and spin them into this page turning novel. She always leaves the readers wondering which part of her story is truth and what might be fiction. MrPerfect.com, takes us into the trials of marriage, the loneliness of divorce and the horror of being in the hands of a serial killer. Dawn's only hope is to escape the madman and the wilderness of Montana. Both proving to be deadly.

K. D. now resides in Arizona with her husband, a Goldendoodle named Fuzzy and a Labradoodle lovingly named, Muddy Brown Dog.

Made in the USA
Lexington, KY
09 December 2014